The feeling of ... against
April's cheek gave her a sense
of peace and being cared for.

But what was even wilder than that thought was
the idea that whatever evil lingered in her past
couldn't harm her while she was guarded by this
Texas Ranger. The terror of her nightmare had
vanished the instant he had taken her into his
arms.

Although he had reluctantly told her about his
family, she wanted to know more about him.
What was his favorite food? What kind of music
did he like? What was his ex-wife like? How
long had he been divorced? And why wasn't
there a woman with him now?

Considering April had no memory, she ought to
be wondering about her own past. Instead she
was obsessing about Rafe's. She needed to think
about something else besides how attracted she
was to a certain Texas Ranger.

Dear Reader,

This is it, the final month of our wonderful three-month celebration of Intimate Moments' fifteenth anniversary. It's been quite a ride, but it's not over yet. For one thing, look who's leading off the month: Rachel Lee, with *Cowboy Comes Home,* the latest fabulous title in her irresistible CONARD COUNTY miniseries. This one has everything you could possibly want in a book, including all the deep emotion Rachel is known for. Don't miss it.

And the rest of the month lives up to that wonderful beginning, with books from both old favorites and new names sure to become favorites. Merline Lovelace's *Return to Sender* will have you longing to work at the post office (I'm not kidding!), while Marilyn Tracy returns to the wonderful (but fictional, darn it!) town of Almost, Texas, with *Almost Remembered.* Look for our TRY TO REMEMBER flash to guide you to Leann Harris's *Trusting a Texan,* a terrific amnesia book, and the EXPECTANTLY YOURS flash marking Raina Lynn's second book, *Partners in Parenthood.* And finally, don't miss *A Hard-Hearted Man,* by brand-new author Melanie Craft. *Your* heart will melt—guaranteed.

And that's not all. Because we're not stopping with the fifteen years behind us. There are that many—and more!—in our future, and I know you'll want to be here for every one. So come back next month, when the excitement and the passion continue, right here in Silhouette Intimate Moments.

Yours,

Leslie J. Wainger
Executive Senior Editor

Please address questions and book requests to:
Silhouette Reader Service
U.S.: 3010 Walden Ave., P.O. Box 1325, Buffalo, NY 14269
Canadian: P.O. Box 609, Fort Erie, Ont. L2A 5X3

TRUSTING A TEXAN

LEANN HARRIS

Silhouette®
INTIMATE™MOMENTS®

Published by Silhouette Books

America's Publisher of Contemporary Romance

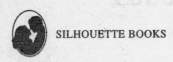

SILHOUETTE BOOKS

ISBN 0-373-07868-4

TRUSTING A TEXAN

Books by Leann Harris

Silhouette Intimate Moments

Bride on the Run #516
Angel at Risk #618
Trouble in Texas #664
Undercover Husband #719
Temporary Marriage #821
Trusting a Texan #868

LEANN HARRIS

When Leann Harris first met her husband in college, she never dreamed she would marry him. After all, he was getting a Ph.D. in the one science she'd managed to avoid—physics! So much for first impressions. They have been happily married for twenty-one years. After graduating from the University of Texas at Austin, Leann taught math and science to deaf high school students until the birth of her first child. It wasn't until her youngest child started school that Leann decided to fulfill a lifelong dream and began writing. She presently lives in Plano, Texas, with her husband and two children.

I would like to thank the following people for their help and expertise. Any errors are mine.

Theresa McKinely Zumwalt, for her knowledge of West Texas, Rangers, horses and ranching.

Lieutenant Dave Davis, for his help with missing persons reports and other police-related matters.

Dr. David Pate, for his help in treating a leg wound.

Chapter 1

Rafael Sanchez pushed back his Stetson, stood in the stirrups of his saddle, and surveyed the valley below him. The air smelled fresh and clean after the morning downpour. But the spring shower had brought several flash floods with it, and Rafe was riding the range to check on his cattle.

A sound like a moan was carried on the wind. Rafe went still and carefully studied the land around him. A small patch of yellow by the highway caught his eye and Rafe wondered if that was the source of the sound. There were no bushes or flowers blooming this time of year that could account for the color.

He guided his mount down the rocky hill. As he got closer, he was able to make out that the telltale yellow was a piece of cloth. He glanced around the horizon to see if there was anything else that seemed out of place.

Nothing.

A chill raced over Rafe's skin that had nothing to do with the wind. Something was wrong.

When he realized the yellow material covered a body—a woman's—he hurried his horse's descent and dismounted a few feet away. She was lying face down, and he couldn't see her face. As he approached, he noticed her blonde hair—almost as golden as the jacket—spread out against the rock.

She moaned.

"Hello," Rafe said, kneeling beside her. "Miss, are you hurt?" He reached out and lightly touched her shoulder. "Miss?"

She opened her eyes and tried to look at him. Then her eyes fluttered closed and a grimace of pain crossed her face. She tried to roll onto her back, but another moan escaped her mouth and she rested her forehead again on the ground.

"Don't move," he warned, then stood, walked to his horse, and unhooked his canteen. Untying the bandanna around his neck, he wet it. His rough fingers touched her cheek as he wiped the cloth over her skin. She grabbed his wrist and guided it toward her temple. He couldn't see the area since it was next to the ground, but under his fingers Rafe felt a lump.

Her eyes fluttered open. "Thank you." She tried to move again. This time Rafe helped her roll over onto her back. He wasn't prepared for the beautiful face that greeted him. She was the type of woman who made men stop and look a second time, and then fantasize. Definitely not politically correct, but a man would have to be dead not to notice her, not to be tempted to fantasize about her. And he wasn't dead by a long stretch.

He lifted his bandanna and saw the dark welt with

several tracks of blood that had run down the side of her face. He lightly wiped away the blood.

"Do you hurt anywhere else beside your head?" he asked.

A puzzled frown crossed her face. "I don't think so."

Rafe's gaze met hers. "Let me check." He waited for her permission.

"Okay."

He moved his hands over her arms and legs, ignoring the wet fabric, looking for any other injuries, but found nothing until he got to her left ankle. When his fingers touched it, a gasp escaped her mouth.

"Sorry," he said, looking at her. In her eyes he could see the pain. Carefully, and with the lightest of touches, he ran his fingers back over the ankle. "It looks as if you've hurt your ankle pretty bad. I don't know if it's broken, but I'll take you to the doctor and make sure."

He sat back on his haunches and pointed to her head. "Besides, you need the doc to take a look at your head."

She nodded, then bit her lip. Rafe didn't wait for a response, but handed the bandanna to her and then stood.

"Where are you going?" she asked, a hint of panic in her voice.

He squatted, bringing his face level with hers again, and took off his Stetson so she would feel more comfortable with him. "I plan to put you on my horse. But it will be easier on both of us if I bring him to you instead of the other way around."

"Oh."

He nodded, put his hat back on, then fetched his horse from where he'd left him. Bending down, he slid his arms around her back and under her knees, and stood. Her body slipped in his arms, and he had to readjust his hold on her. She grimaced in pain. "Sorry," he whispered.

She gave him an anemic smile.

"Put your arms around my neck," he commanded her. And she complied.

Rafe lifted her to the saddle. With one hand on the saddle horn and the other wrapped around her waist, he slipped his boot in the stirrup and hauled himself up, lifting her slightly so he could slide into the saddle beneath her. He readjusted her in his lap, being careful not to bump her ankle. "Are you comfortable?" he asked.

She nodded.

Damn, he wished *he* were. His body had suddenly sprung to life at the feel of her bottom fitting snugly against him. He was a professional lawman, for Pete's sake, trying to help this woman. So why was his body acting like a youth's with his hormones raging out of control?

Rafe turned his horse and started up the hill. The angle forced the woman against him and he felt every inch of her wet, lovely body molded to his, adding to his awareness of her. As if he needed reminding.

From the condition of her clothes and hair, it was obvious that she'd been caught out in the storm. A shiver ran through her. He slid his arm around her waist, trying to offer what warmth he could.

"I'll get you wet," she protested weakly.

"Don't worry. When I get you back to the ranch, I'll get you some dry clothes before I take you to see the doctor."

"Th-that sounds wonderful."

His mind kept drifting to the feel of her against him. Finally, when his brain kicked into gear, he asked,

"How did you manage to get yourself caught in the flash flood we had this morning?"

She threw him a puzzled frown. "What?"

"What were you doing out in the storm? And how did you get out to this remote area?" He looked over the rugged land that he called home. "I didn't see a car or a horse anywhere near where I found you."

She remained quiet for a minute, then bit her lip. "I don't remember."

Goose bumps raced over his skin. "What do you mean, you don't remember?" His voice sounded harsher than he intended.

Her gaze met his and her growing panic was clearly reflected in her green eyes. "I mean, I don't know what I was doing out there this morning."

Rafe's first reaction was to yell what did she mean she didn't know. It wouldn't do her or him any good if he scared her witless. "Well," he said, swallowing his uneasiness, "tell me what you remember and we'll go from there."

She stared out at the horizon. He watched her teeth worry her full bottom lip. His body tightened at the sight.

"What were you doing out this morning?" he asked, hoping his gentle questioning would jog her memory. "Did you come on foot or did you have a horse or car stashed someplace close by?"

She shook her head. "I don't remember." Shyly, she glanced at him.

Rafe didn't like the direction this conversation was moving. "What *do* you remember?"

She closed her eyes and her brow furrowed in a frown. "Nothing." There was panic in her voice.

"Nothing?"

Her bottom lip quivered. "Everything's a blank...before I woke up and saw you."

The image of his being her only memory burned in his brain. "A hell of a thing to have as your only memory." A deep laugh rumbled in his chest.

Her gaze locked with his and a jolt of electricity arced between them. He glanced away and fixed his eyes on the hills before them. He had found a woman, nearly drowned, bum ankle, and no memory—and suddenly his body wanted hers. His timing was really rotten. So what else was new?

It took a good fifteen minutes to cover the ground between where he found her by the highway and the ranch house. When they rode into his yard, a sigh of relief escaped her lips. Her teeth were chattering and her body shook. He slipped off the horse, then gathered her into his arms.

"You have a l-lovely home," she commented as he climbed the steps to the porch.

"Thanks." Rafe was proud of the ranch house that his great-uncle had built. Successive generations had added to the rambling house and updated it. In his great-uncle's den there were pictures of the cavalry unit to which he had belonged. There was also a computer hooked up to the Internet, a laser printer, and a fax machine. Rafe might live out in the Llano Estacado, miles away from any civilization, but he was still in touch with the modern world. He had to be when he was working for the Texas Rangers.

Stopping before the screen door, he waited. "My hands are kinda full," he finally said. "You want to open the door for us?"

"Oh." She grasped the handle and pulled it open. Rafe shouldered the screen further open, then waited for her to open the wooden door. It swung into the building. Going directly to the bathroom, he eased her down onto the closed toilet, then stepped back and handed her a towel.

"Why don't you get out of those wet things and—" he turned and pulled his bathrobe off the hook "—use my robe to cover up." She took the robe from his hands, clutching it as if it were a lifeline. Nodding toward the door, he said, "I'll wait out in the hall. If you have any problems, yell."

"Okay."

He stepped out, closing the door behind him. He was tempted to call the clinic and alert them that he had a patient with a lump on the side of her head, no memory, and an ankle with at least a bad sprain. But Rafe decided that it would be unwise to leave his find by herself for too long. He took off his hat and hung it on the coat tree in the corner of the living room, then went back to wait by the bathroom door.

She stared at the closed door for several moments, fighting the panic that pounded through her brain. When she had awakened a while ago, her life had been a total and complete blank. She couldn't even come up with a name.

She pulled herself to a standing position and glanced into the mirror, hoping that seeing her reflection might help her memory. The woman who stared back at her was a stranger. The image brought no memories.

She bit her lip and struggled against the tears that threatened to overflow. Nothing was going to be accomplished by standing here and feeling sorry for herself, she thought. With the towel, she dried her hair and face, then removed her shirt and bra and dried her upper body.

Unzipping her jeans, she worked them and her panties down to her knees, then shrugged on the robe. She sat on the closed toilet seat and removed her tennis shoes. She inched the jeans off her uninjured leg, but as she tried to slip the material off her other ankle, the pain stopped her efforts.

Pausing for a moment, she tightened the terry belt around her waist. The smell of man wafted up from the material. She recognized the scent as that of her rescuer, and on some basic level, it calmed her nerves.

"Huh—" She tried to hail him back into the room, but realized she didn't know his name. "I'm ready," she called out.

The bathroom door opened and he reentered. He was a solid, reassuring presence in this nightmare she was having—a handsome man, tall, with dark, wavy hair and brown eyes that a woman could get lost in.

"I was able to get everything off except—" She looked down at her jeans bunched around her ankle. "I got them that far but I need your help to get them off my injured foot."

He kneeled before her and carefully pulled her jeans and panties over her foot, setting them on the edge of the tub. Seeing him handle her lingerie brought a blush to her cheeks and an odd feeling to her middle.

"What's your name?" she asked as he worked.

He looked up, surprise coloring his eyes. His black hair waved around his ears and a lock fell onto his forehead. His olive skin glowed with health and vigor.

"When I called you a moment ago, I realized I don't know your name." A strained laugh followed. "For that matter, I don't know my name, either."

His large hand rested on her knee. The robe slid open and his skin touched hers. It was as if an electrical current had run through her body. As if burned, he quickly drew his hand back.

"Don't worry about it." As a reassurance, it lacked a certain conviction. "I'm sure your condition is only temporary." He glanced away.

"And your name is?" she asked again, wanting to put a name to her rescuer.

He looked back at her and held out his hand. "Rafael Sanchez, part-time rancher and full-time Texas Ranger."

She might not know who she was, but she knew that if he was a Ranger, he'd take care of her. Probably the best thing that could've happened to her was to be found by a Ranger. Rangers were tough, independent men who were instrumental in bringing law to the Texas frontier a hundred years ago. And if he was a Ranger, that meant she was somewhere in Texas.

She slid her hand into his and his fingers curled around hers. Warmth flooded her stomach. "I guess if I had to wake up without a memory, having you find me was a stroke of good luck." She tried to sound positive, but she couldn't keep the nervousness out of her voice.

"Don't worry about your memory. I don't know much about amnesia, but I'm sure yours will come around soon. The bump on your head might be the cause of your problem."

She tried to stand, but he swept her up into his arms. The darn robe parted again, giving him a generous view of her legs. His gaze clashed with hers and she saw—there in his eyes—his awareness of her as a woman. With heart pounding, she grabbed the edges and held them closed.

"Would you like for me to get you one of my T-shirts to wear under the robe?" he asked.

"Yes."

He gently set her back on the toilet seat and disappeared from the bathroom, returning moments later with a T-shirt and some running shorts. Handing them to her, he stepped out into the hall. "Call me when you're ready."

She nodded and quickly slipped off the robe and put on the shirt and the shorts. But a chill swept over her, and she reached for the robe again.

"I'm ready," she called out.

Instantly, Rafe was back in the room. His brow arched in surprise.

"I was cold."

He scooped her up in his arms and started out of the room.

"You don't have to carry me," she protested. Of course, she wondered why she had even spoken. The surety of Rafe's arms around her made her feel better.

"Until we know about your ankle, why don't you let me carry you?"

He stated it so reasonably that all she could do was nod her permission.

Rafe walked down the hall through the living room and into the kitchen. He stopped by the back door. "You want to grab my keys?" He nodded toward the nail by the door. She noticed that he avoided looking directly at her.

Reaching out, she grabbed the keys and wrapped her fingers around the cold metal. Rafe made his way out into the garage, and placed her in the passenger seat of his truck. She handed him the keys and his skin brushed hers, sending a shiver up her arm.

"I'll need to get my hat. I'll be back in a minute." He reemerged moments later wearing his off-white Stetson, looking like an official Texas Ranger. It was a comforting sight.

He stopped and leaned in the driver's side of the truck. "Give me five minutes to unsaddle my horse."

She nodded, and watched him untie his horse from the fence and lead him into the barn.

What was wrong with her to feel this attraction to a stranger? The fact was, she was a stranger to herself. She looked at her ring finger. There was nothing there, and no tan line to indicate she might have worn a ring. But for all she knew, she might be married with a dozen kids waiting at home for her, so she definitely had no business reacting to him this way.

Rafael appeared several minutes later and hopped into the truck. He didn't say anything on the trip into town, but she could see the frown that creased his brow. His mind must be filled with as many questions as hers, she thought.

"Where are we going?" she asked.

"The nearest medical help is in Saddle. The doc there is a trained E.R. doctor who moved out here after she married one of the deputies."

"What county are we in?"

"Brewster. 6,193 square miles. Bigger than Connecticut, Rhode Island, New Jersey and Delaware."

"Big Bend." The words were out of her mouth before she was conscious she'd said them.

His eyebrow arched. "Yeah, Big Bend National Park is in the southern part of the county. Do you remember anything else?"

She shook her head. "I don't even know how I knew that."

"Could be you're a Texan. Most people in the state know of Big Bend and what county it's in."

"How do you figure that?"

"You sound like a Texan."

It wasn't much, but at least it was a thin thread to hold on to.

He glanced at her. "Does this scenery do anything for your memory?" he asked.

She stared at the rugged peaks in the distance, but nothing came to mind. Not so much as a glimmer. "No." There was a wealth of defeat in her answer.

"Well, my educated guess is that you either live in Alpine, or you were visiting someone around Saddle."

"Why do you think that?"

"Because I know everyone in Saddle. Also, I found you on one of the county roads, not near the interstate, so that would mean you were probably not just driving through. I'll call around later and see if anyone was expecting you."

"Sounds reasonable to me." It also sounded reassuring. It appeared that Rafe didn't plan on deserting her. She fiddled with the edges of the bathrobe, unwilling to let him see her reaction.

They fell silent for the rest of the ten-minute trip into Saddle. It was a small community made up of three streets. Two streets were residential, and the other was business: a gas station, restaurant, post office, sheriff's office and feed store. Rafe pulled up to the first brick building and parked. A small sign by the door read "Clinic." He came around, opened her door and swept her up in his arms. He carried her inside and nodded to the man and woman sitting in the waiting room.

"Hi, Marv, Sarah. How's your son doing at college?"

"He loves the big city," Marv answered.

Rafe stopped and looked at the older man. Lubbock—a big city? Well, he guessed, compared to Saddle, it was.

Rafe grinned. "Well, tell George not to speed. The high-way patrol out around there are always looking for college kids."

The couple looked expectantly at Rafe to introduce them to the woman in his arms. But he smiled politely, then walked down the short hall. As they passed the closed door of the examining room, it opened and two people emerged: a woman in a lab coat and a young man probably about sixteen.

"Rafe, what are you doing here?" the woman in the lab coat asked.

A grin curved Rafe's generous mouth. "I brought you a patient."

"What a nice thing for a brother to do." The doctor stepped away from the door and motioned them inside. "Why don't you wait in there while I talk to Ben's parents?"

Rafe nodded and entered the room, setting his patient on the examining table.

"That's your sister?" she asked, amazement in her voice.

"Yup." The greatest surprise of Rafe's life was when his mom passed away eighteen months ago and he found, among her things, the name of his father. Finally, after several months of cursing the man and being angry at his callous behavior, curiosity had gotten the best of Rafe. He had confronted George Anderson at his Midland office. News that he'd fathered a son came first as a shock to the intrepid oilman, then as a delight.

Coincidentally, one of Rafe's sisters had just moved to Saddle and married the deputy stationed there. For Rafe, who'd been raised as the only child of a single woman, having a family came as a mixed blessing.

His charge leaned forward, expecting more of an explanation. "And?"

He rested his hip on the cabinet opposite the examining table. "And what?"

Before she had the opportunity to answer, the doctor came back into the room. She paused just inside the door, studying first her patient, then Rafe. "Okay, Rafe, what can I do for you two?"

"This lady needs to be examined," he answered, knowing that Dr. Alexandra Grey would want a more detailed answer.

Alex didn't move from the door. She folded her arms across her chest and waited.

"After the flash floods we had this morning, I went looking for any stray cattle that might have been caught in the flood. I spotted Jane Doe here by the road."

"Jane Doe?" Alex asked, surprise in her voice.

He nodded. "The lady doesn't remember anything before she woke up and saw me crouching over her."

Alex shook her head. "What a shock to have you as her first memory." Her mouth turned up in a grin. She moved toward the examining table. "Any other injuries I should know about?"

Rafe pointed toward her head. "Aside from that bad-looking bump on her head, she has a swollen ankle. I think it's just a sprain, not broken."

"Okay. Why don't you wait in my office while I examine our Jane Doe." Alex waited until her brother was out of the room, then turned back to her patient. She held out her hand. "I'm Dr. Alexandra Grey, Rafe's sister."

The woman on the table shook the doctor's hand. "It's nice to meet you, Dr. Grey. I wish I could tell you my name, but...I don't know what it is." She shrugged her shoulders.

"Well, let's take care of that. Rafe called you Jane Doe, but you don't look like a Jane Doe." She rubbed her chin and pursed her lips. "Let's see, Sheila? Bridget? No, Madeline." She paused to see if she got any reaction from her patient. "That's not it, either." Alexandra stroked her chin, her gaze falling on the calendar hanging on the wall. "April." She looked at her patient. "April—it fits you."

The woman nodded. "I like that."

"Well, April, let's check out your head and ankle. Do you think that you're injured anywhere else?"

April shook her head. "I don't think so."

"All right. Let's have a look."

Rafe paced around Alex's office. He stopped by the door and looked across the hall at the examining room door. Before he could turn away, the door opened and Alex emerged.

"I need to x-ray April's ankle. I have a wheelchair in the storeroom."

"Her name is April?" Rafe asked, looking over Alex's shoulder to the woman he'd found. "She remembered what she was doing on my land?"

Alex's expression could only be termed long-suffering. "No, she hasn't regained her memory."

"Then why did you call her April?" Rafe's gaze moved from his sister to his charge.

"Because neither she nor I thought she looked like a Jane Doe."

His eyes widened.

"Don't give me that look," his sister replied.

"April," he murmured. His gaze shifted from his sister to the beautiful, blond woman wearing his robe.

"Rafe, sometimes you have the soul of a heathen," Alex commented.

"I might be a heathen," he told his sister, "but that doesn't change the fact that I'm a damned good cop."

Alex grinned. "I didn't doubt it."

Twenty minutes later they were seated in Alex's office. "Okay, April here has a mild concussion and a badly sprained ankle. But other than that, there aren't any other physical problems that I can see."

"Aside from not knowing who she is and not knowing anything about her past."

Alex gave her brother a dirty look. "Thank you for pointing that out, brother of mine."

"Well, do you have any idea when her memory will return?"

Folding her hands on her desk, Alex smiled at April. "No. It could return as soon as tomorrow or it could never return."

"Terrific," Rafe grumbled.

A trace of panic appeared in April's eyes. Alex smiled, trying to reassure her patient. "Most people regain their lost memory. Very few people remain cut off from their past." She looked at Rafe. "She'll need to stay off that ankle for a while, keep it elevated. Tomorrow, heat on the ankle will speed up the healing. I have some crutches that I can lend April to help her get around." She rose and disappeared into the storage room, reemerging a few moments later with a set of crutches.

"Thanks," Rafe replied.

Alex leaned against her desk. "Since April doesn't

know who she is or where she was going, we'd better consider where she's going to recuperate.''

"Could she stay with you?" Rafe asked his sister.

"The baby has just come down with chicken pox. It wouldn't be a good idea to expose April to that now. Maybe she could stay with the Greggs out at their ranch.''

A look of panic crossed April's face. "I thought I might...." Her words trailed off as both Alex and Rafe looked at her. "Uh, I mean...I thought I could stay with you.'' She nodded toward Rafe.

There was such hope in her eyes that he couldn't turn her down, even though his body was acting up. He was old enough to control himself. "If April would feel comfortable at my ranch, that's fine with me.''

A smile appeared on April's face, the first that Alex had seen since she'd met the woman. It was as if some unknown tension had left April's body and she had relaxed. Well, the two of them certainly seemed comfortable together, Alex thought. As a matter of fact, Alex had never seen her normally taciturn brother more animated than he had been in the last hour.

Alex met her brother's gaze and her eyebrow arched. "Then we have that problem solved." Alex turned to April. "Do you need something to wear?"

"My things were wet, and I left them at Rafe's house,'' April answered, gazing at her hands folded in her lap.

"Well, if you need anything—nightgown, robe, girl things—just call," Alex told her. "I think we're probably the same size. Rafe, you're going to need to keep an eye on April for the next few hours. If she gets sleepy or drowsy, call. She needs to stay awake to make sure everything is okay.''

Rafe stood and handed the crutches to April. When she placed them under her arms, the robe—his robe—gapped open to the waist, allowing him a generous view of her legs.

"Maybe April would like to borrow the bottoms of some scrubs so she can use the crutches," Alex commented. "She might feel more comfortable."

Rafe nodded and April gave her a smile of gratitude.

"All right, I'll get them and take them into the examining room where you can change."

Five minutes later, April emerged from the examining room dressed in the blue bottoms, but she still had on Rafe's T-shirt. It was obvious she didn't have anything on underneath.

Alex glanced at Rafe. "Maybe I should get April a scrub *top*, too."

He felt like he'd been punched in the gut.

"I'd appreciate that," April said, blushing.

Alex retrieved the top and handed it to April. While April changed, the doctor studied her brother. "You certainly have your work cut out for you," she commented.

Rafe shrugged. "I've had harder tasks."

Before she could respond, April emerged from the exam room dressed in the scrubs, Rafe's clothes in her hands.

"You look very professional," Alex declared. "Could be you are in the health field. What do you think, Rafe?"

"I think you make a better doctor than a detective," he answered, stepping around her and grabbing his hat.

"Sometimes Rafael, you remind me so much of Dad, it's scary."

He grimaced—he was still touchy about his relationship to George Anderson—then looked at April. "Ready to go?"

"Yes."

"Is your husband in his office?" Rafe asked Alex as he followed April out of the building.

"I think so, but I haven't talked to him since this morning."

"We'll stop by and see him." Rafe opened the truck door for April and lifted her onto the seat.

"Who is her husband?" April asked.

"Derek's the deputy sheriff assigned to Saddle."

April went deathly pale.

Chapter 2

April's reaction peaked Rafe's curiosity. The drive from the clinic to the sheriff's office took less than a minute, and they were the only vehicle moving on the street. After parking the truck, Rafe walked around it, then opened her door.

"If you'll hand me the crutches, I'll help you with them."

She hesitated, then slowly handed them to him.

Rafe felt a need to explain, to try to ease the strain he saw in her eyes. "Since we're here, I thought we'd talk to the deputy to see if there is a report on a missing woman fitting your description. Although I have the same information at my ranch, it's always better to have more than one set of eyes looking for clues."

Her reluctance showed as clearly on her face as did the sun rising over the Davis Mountains each morning. She glanced down at her lap. Past experience had taught him that the main reason most people were wary of the police was because they'd run afoul of the law.

"Is there some reason why we shouldn't check with Derek?" he asked.

Her head jerked up. "Is this necessary?" she asked, which only added to his suspicions.

That sixth sense that cops develop began to yell at him that there was trouble here that had nothing to do with the woman's memory loss.

Or maybe it did.

She looked down at the blue scrubs and bare feet. "I'm not exactly dressed to go visiting." She looked pleased that she had come up with a reason.

The corners of his mouth turned up in a grin. "Don't worry about it. Derek's only concern will be about what happened. Besides, Derek's one fine cop, the best at what he does. With him on the job, our chances of finding out who you are are much better."

He held out his hand, waiting to help her down to the ground. With a minimum of fuss, she slipped out the door and allowed him to place a crutch under each arm.

The deputy was seated at the desk, talking on the phone. The instant they entered the office, he smiled and said into the receiver, "They're here. I'll talk to you later at home, sweetheart." He hung up and stood.

"I take it that was Alex on the other end," Rafe said to the deputy as he closed the door behind him.

"Yup." He smiled and held out his hand to April. "I'm Derek Grey, deputy sheriff assigned to Saddle. And you must be April. My wife just told me about you."

Despite Derek's grin and friendly demeanor, April hesitated to take his hand. She gave him a painful smile and stepped backward toward Rafe.

Derek looked at Rafe, questions in his eyes.

Shrugging, Rafe helped April into one of the chairs in front of the desk. He sat in the other one and took off his Stetson.

"I take it that Alex told you about April's memory loss. We came here to see if there was a report of a missing woman who fits April's description. I know it's kinda early, but there's no reason not to check."

Derek turned and pulled a file from the bookcase behind the desk. "Yesterday, the Department of Public Safety put out the new list of missing persons." He opened the folder and sat down. "Let's see—" His thumb ran down the list. "Do you know what kind of car she was driving?"

Rafe shook his head. "Nope. I found her at the edge of my land near County Road 4. There wasn't a car in sight, but there had been a flash flood this morning in that section of road. That's why I was out—riding the range, looking for stock in trouble."

Derek nodded. "I'll drive out there later today and look for the vehicle." He resumed scanning the list. "Female, five foot four or five, blond hair, green eyes, late twenties, early thirties." His finger rested on the line as he glanced up and looked into April's eyes.

"I'm five-six," April added. Her eyes widened as if the information surprised her.

Derek finished the list, then handed it to Rafe. "I don't see anyone fitting her description."

Quickly, Rafe surveyed the list. Nothing. "It will help when we find her car. We can track her through it."

"If anything comes in, I'll call you."

"Okay," Rafe answered.

"Why don't we take the lady's fingerprints and run them through the state database? Maybe something will show up there.'' Derek turned to April. ''Is it okay with you if we take your prints?''

Rafe wondered if April would object to the procedure. Only criminals and state employees were kept in the state's computer. Combined with her reaction to the sheriff, it might be a clue to her identity.

''Yes, it's fine with me.'' There was no hesitation in her voice, no shadow in her eyes. ''Anything that will help find out who I am.''

Derek nodded and motioned for April to follow him.

Well, so much for that theory, Rafe thought. He followed them to the corner of the office where bookings were done. The first time Derek did the printing, April's fingerprints were smudged and unreadable.

''Do most fingerprints turn out like that?'' April asked, pointing to the black blur on the page.

''No,'' Rafe said, handing her a paper towel.

Derek looked at Rafe.

April picked up on the silent communication. ''What is it?'' she asked, a note of panic in her voice.

''Whatever job you do, you must handle a lot of paper,'' Rafe answered.

She looked at her hands and frowned. ''Why do you say that?''

''Your fingerprints aren't readable. They've been worn down. People who handle a lot of paper have that problem when fingerprinted. Let's try a little glycerin on your skin and see if we can get a clear print.''

April looked from one man to the other, then held out her hands. Rafe put several drops of glycerin on her fingertips and then gently rubbed it in. It was a uniquely sensual experience for him. All sorts of emotions ran through him that had never happened at a booking before. When he realized where his thoughts had drifted, he yanked them back. "Let's try this again." He glanced up and saw Derek grinning at him.

They repeated the printing, this time with success.

"Where are you going to keep April?" Derek asked after he faxed the prints to Austin.

April tensed.

"I thought I'd take her back to my ranch for the time being. That would be the easiest all around with your baby being sick." Rafe felt April relax.

A knowing look entered Derek's eyes. "You're right."

Putting on his hat, Rafe stood and helped April to her feet, then handed her the crutches. She struggled out the door to his truck. After helping her into the cab and closing the door, Rafe leaned through the window. "I forgot to tell Derek something. I'll just be a moment."

He stepped back up onto the sidewalk and leaned through the door of the office. Derek, who was reviewing the missing persons' reports, looked up.

"After you check the wanted posters and the APB's, let me know what you find."

Setting the sheets back on the desk, Derek asked, "You think I'm going to discover something?"

A weary sigh escaped Rafe's mouth. "Yeah. I've got that nagging feeling that the lady's in trouble."

"All right. I'll let you know how everything turns out."

Just as Rafe climbed into the cab of the truck, April's stomach rumbled. Her hand clamped over her waist, and she shot Rafe an embarrassed smile.

"I couldn't have said it better, myself," he commented, inserting the key into the ignition. "I'm starved." Glancing at his watch, he noted the time was

close to two. "You have your choice. I can take you
back to my ranch and feed you a bologna sandwich with
stale chips, or we could drive down the street and have
lunch at Mabel's." He pretended to do some deep thinking before he added with a grin. "Let's see, it's Thursday, which means Mabel is serving fried chicken and
Red Velvet cake. If that woman was ten years younger,
I'd ask her to marry me. Of course, she probably
wouldn't want an uncivilized lawman like me."

His comment had the desired result: April grinned.
"Her cooking is that good?"

"Mabel's got more blue ribbons from the state fair
than the rest of the women in this county and the next
combined."

"Oh, my. Well, you certainly make Mabel's sound as
good as dining at The Mansion."

"The Mansion?" he repeated, knowing the restaurant
she spoke of, but checking to see if *she* knew.

"The Mansion in Dallas." The words rolled off her
tongue before she had time to think. Her startled gaze
flew to his. "I don't know how I knew that."

Unable to help himself, he grabbed her hand and
gently squeezed it. His skin burned at the contact.
Quickly, he released it. "It's a good sign, April. It's kind
of like your memory's been dammed up and there are
fissures in the wall, allowing bits of your past to trickle
through. With time, all your memory should return."

She frowned at him. "I just wish I could remember
now."

"Don't worry. Trust me, I'll take good care of you."

"Okay." The awe in her voice caused her to go still.
Her gaze flew to his. "I do trust you," she said again,
more forcefully.

He pushed back his white Stetson and smiled at her.

Although he'd helped her this morning, what had happened thus far didn't warrant the level of trust that she was putting in him. There was something else at work here. Something that even she didn't recognize. "Well, if you trust me, then I recommend we eat at Mabel's. It'll be the best meal you've had in a long time."

She glanced down at her scrubs and bare feet. "I'm willing if she won't mind my attire."

A grin curved his mouth at the cultured word. "Attire?"

She blushed.

"There's another clue, April. You speak with an elegant tone. I would've said my duds or *ropa*—that's Spanish for clothes."

She frowned at him. "I don't know."

"Who's the detective here?"

A blush crept up her neck.

"Trust me, April. Most of the folks around here don't use 'attire.' Your using it helps put you from an urban area, probably from the eastern part of the state."

"How can you be sure that I'm a Texan?"

He rested his wrists on the steering wheel. "Because of the way you sound. I know a Texan when I hear one. Your drawl is dainty, but it's definitely there."

Shrugging, she looked out the window. "Okay. Let's go eat at Mabel's."

He put the truck in gear and drove a few blocks down the street, parking in front of a two-story brick building. Hopping out, he raced around the front of the truck, opened April's door, and scooped her up in his arms.

"What are you doing?" she demanded.

His body reacted to her nearness—anyone would think he was an untried teenager with his first crush. He swallowed the lump in his throat and tried to ignore the womanly scent of her. "Taking you inside. Mabel won't let you inside without shoes, but we'll appeal to her soft heart if I carry you."

Reluctantly, she put her arms around his neck. Rafe cursed under his breath, questioning the wisdom of his move. He was already acutely aware of April. He didn't need an up-close-and-personal reminder of how her nearness affected him. He stopped at the door. "We've done this before. My hands are full, you want to open the door?"

She grinned at him, causing his heart to skip a beat. "Of course." She pulled the glass door open, allowing him to slip inside.

"I'll be there in a moment," a voice from the kitchen called.

"We'll seat ourselves, Mabel," Rafe answered.

Before he could place April in a chair, a woman appeared at the kitchen door. Mabel might only be five foot, but with her bottled red hair and orthopedic shoes, she was a force to be dealt with. "What are you doing, Rafe?" She strolled to the table.

Rafe couldn't prevent the guilty flush that appeared on his cheeks. "I'm helping April to her chair."

"She can't walk herself?" Mabel shot back.

"Nope. She sprained her ankle this morning."

Before he could explain more, Mabel jumped in. "I'm sorry to hear that. You take her to see Dr. Alex?"

"Yes."

She turned back to April and introduced herself.

"It's a pleasure to meet you, Mabel. Rafe says you make the best chicken in this part of the state. I'm looking forward to it."

Mabel threw Rafe a satisfied glance. "The boy always

had a lot of sense." She carefully surveyed April's scrubs, then looked at Rafe, waiting for an explanation.

"April was caught in a flash flood this morning at the edge of my land. Alex loaned the scrubs to her until her clothes dry."

"I see. Well, I take it you two want something to eat."

"You're a mind reader," Rafe replied, with a grin.

She scowled at him. "That's not what my ex used to say." She disappeared into the kitchen. "Rafe," she called out from the kitchen. "You get yourself and April some tea."

"Yes, ma'am."

Two plastic cups and a pitcher appeared on the window ledge that looked into the kitchen. Rafe stood and poured them tea and carried the cups back to the table.

"I hope you like sweetened tea. Mabel doesn't serve it any other way."

"I think so," April replied, taking the cup from him. A large grin curved her lips.

"What are you smiling at?" he asked, resuming his seat.

"You."

"What about me?"

"You did Mabel's bidding mighty quickly."

A sparkle entered his eye. "You've never seen Mabel riled. It's easier to do what she says. Besides, I'd do just about anything—legal, that is—for Mabel's fried chicken."

A cloud passed over April's face and her eyes darkened.

"What is it?"

Her head jerked up and she met his gaze. "I don't

know. It's like someone stepped on my grave. I felt cold.''

Rafe racked his brain, trying to recall what he'd said. He'd been teasing her about doing anything legal for Mabel's chicken.

"How long have you lived out here?" April asked, her fingers skimming the outside of her glass.

Her question drew him out of his musings. "I've been assigned to this part of the state since '90, but I grew up in the Valley. Then after college, I joined the Highway Patrol.''

"And how did you become a Ranger?"

"In '87, there were openings in the Rangers, so I took the exam. I was one of the first Hispanic Rangers.''

A small frown crinkled her brow. "But how could Dr. Alex be your sister?" Her *faux pas* ringing in the air, a blush stained her cheeks. "I mean...uh...."

A laugh rumbled in his chest. "It was a surprise to me, too, to discover I had sisters.''

"Sisters?"

"Three. The oldest is a lawyer. Alex, the middle one, is a doctor. And the youngest has a doctorate and teaches in college.''

"But Alex is...uh...you're—" The more she said, the deeper the hole she dug for herself. Rafe took pity on her. "They're my half-sisters. We have the same father, but different mothers. I didn't know a thing about that part of my family until my mother died and I went through her things and discovered my father's name.''

"How did you feel?"

"At first, I felt angry that he'd left my mother pregnant and alone.'' He didn't mention how long it took him to get over the anger. "Eventually, I went to Midland and confronted him.'' His mind wandered back to

that first meeting with his father. "I was news to him.
He never knew that he'd gotten my mom pregnant. At
first, he was stunned, then amazed. But he was thrilled
that he had a son and introduced me to my sisters—and
anyone who'd listen to him.

"It was odd but I already knew Alex before I discovered our relationship. She helped with the TB epidemic
that ran through town last year. She and Derek fell in
love and married. It's bizarre how I grew up in the
Valley and Alex in Midland, and then we ended up in
the same small town in west Texas."

"Here it is," Mabel announced, setting two plates of
steaming, golden, fried chicken before her customers.
April moaned at the exquisite smell.

Rafe grinned. "I think, Mabel, you're about to make
another lifelong customer."

"If this tastes half as good as it smells, you're right,"
agreed April. She pinched a piece of the crispy skin and
popped it into her mouth. "Mmm." April's eyes fluttered closed and a look of ecstasy crossed her face.

Her reaction shot through him like lightning through
thunderclouds, bringing heat and electricity. As Rafe focused on April's expression, all sorts of thoughts raced
through his head—none had anything to do with food.
Then he caught Mabel staring from April to him. When
he looked questioningly at her, she just raised her eyebrow.

"Why don't you join us, Mabel?" Rafe asked. "I was
hoping you'd sit with us while we eat so I could ask
you a couple of questions. I need your help to find out
who April is."

"She doesn't know who she is?" Mabel pulled out a
chair and sat down.

He nodded and turned to April, who hadn't waited for

him, but was biting into her meat. He laughed. "How is it?"

With April's mouth full of chicken, she could only nod.

"Well, if April could speak, I'd let her tell you how I found her this morning lying on the ground next to County Road 4. She'd been caught in the flash flood, but there was no sign of her car or how she got out to that spot. She doesn't have any memory of her life before waking up. I was hoping that maybe you might of heard of someone visiting the area, since your place is the center of information for this part of the county." After taking a swallow of his iced tea, he asked, "Do you know of anyone around here who had a guest or was expecting someone?"

Leaning back in her chair, Mabel rubbed her chin. "Let's see, have I heard of anyone visiting?"

Rafe waited as Mabel reviewed her memory.

"Marv Davis's daughter and granddaughter visited last week—but other than that, I can't think of anyone. Besides, all those college kids away at school won't show up for another month. Everything is pretty normal."

A sigh escaped him. It had been a long shot that Mabel might know. Well, he'd just keep looking.

"Where'd you say you found April?" she asked.

"At the edge of my land just off County Road 4."

"Let's see, the only folks off that road are the Taylors and the Johnsons. Dick's in town, but the Johnsons are out visiting their daughter in Los Angeles."

Mabel crossed her arms and pursed her lips, obviously reviewing her day. "Oh, wait, now that I think about it, I did come across a stranger this morning. He came in just before the lunch rush. All he wanted was coffee."

She pointed to the table in the corner. "He sat there. I did get the feeling he was looking for someone."

"Did he say anything?" Rafe asked.

"Nope. He just watched everyone come and go." Mabel shrugged.

"What did this man look like?"

Mabel flashed him a grin. "Oh, he was a handsome devil, with blond hair and a red mustache. And he had dreamy blue eyes that made...never mind."

Rafe glanced at April to see her reaction. Her face seemed to lose what little animation it had, and she pushed away her remaining chicken. Her look of desolation touched his heart.

"Mabel, I think we're both ready for a piece of that Red Velvet cake of yours."

Mabel hurried into the kitchen and reemerged with two pieces of cake. April took a bite of her dessert. The rich flavor made her close her eyes as she savored the taste.

"This is wonderful, Mabel," April said. "I can see why Rafe raved about your cooking."

Beaming, Mabel refilled both tea glasses. "Well, I always said his momma raised him right." She flashed him a smile.

"Now, if you could only made a good *enchilada,* I'd up and marry you tomorrow."

Mabel grinned. "In your dreams, mister."

Rafe turned to April. "You ready to go?"

"I need a moment before we leave." She glanced around and found the sign she was looking for. Rafe helped her to the bathroom.

"Mabel," Rafe called out. "Why don't you pack me a couple of pieces of the cake. I think April would enjoy a snack later."

"All right," came her reply.

Rafe walked to the window. The information Mabel told them—that there was a stranger in town—bothered him. Not only had April appeared in this remote spot of Texas, but another stranger had turned up this morning, too. Of course, the town of Saddle was on the road to Big Bend National Park, but most tourists—when they stopped—liked to talk. Mabel could get the shiest folks to open up. This particular traveler didn't fit the normal tourist profile.

Rafe had a gnawing suspicion that the two strangers were connected.

He moved to the front door and dialed Derek's office. The deputy picked up on the first ring. "Sheriff's office."

"Derek, this is Rafe. Mabel told me an interesting story about a stranger in her restaurant this morning. He didn't say anything, but sat in the corner, drank coffee, and watched everyone. I wonder if there could be a connection between this stranger and April."

"What do you want me to do?" Derek asked.

"Just keep your eyes peeled. Something's going on here, and I don't want to be caught flat-footed."

"I'll do it."

Rafe hung up the phone. His sixth sense was on alert. Two strangers in one day was one too many. Rangers always were prepared for the unexpected, and this little scenario had all the markings of trouble.

Chapter 3

"Was I right?" Rafe asked as he drove out of town. "Lunch at Mabel's was *muy bueno?*"

The Spanish phrase rolled off his tongue with ease, teasing her hearing and causing an odd fluttering in her heart.

"Indeed, you were right. Mabel is a whiz in the kitchen. I wish I could be as good."

His gaze focused on her face. "You remember?"

Just as it occurred to her that she had said something about her past, the memory slipped away. Blankness faced her again, making her spirits plummet. "No, but it's only natural to be envious of such good cooking."

His large, warm hand rested on her forearm and squeezed. "Don't worry. You're showing positive signs of regaining your memory."

She gave him a wobbly smile. Looking out the truck window, she noticed the mountains in the distance. This was a rugged land that somehow called to her on a basic level. She might not be from around here, but the majesty of the mountains appealed to her.

"What are you thinking?" Rafe asked, glancing at her.

April's fingers played with the hem of her scrub top. "I was just thinking how beautiful this land is."

He threw her a surprised look. "Oh?"

A blush crept up her neck. "Yes."

"That's interesting."

"Why do you say that?" The question rolled off her tongue before she had a chance to think.

His eyes were trained on the road before him. "Well, this part of Texas is sparse and rugged. It doesn't appeal to everyone." He shrugged. "Green's kind of at a premium here."

A thread of hope wrapped around April's heart, contrasting starkly with her earlier despair. Maybe they were onto a clue to her past. She turned to Rafe.

"Well, maybe that's a lead as to who I am."

"Could be." He shot her a look. "But I wouldn't bet *mi madra's* pearls on it."

"What?"

A corner of his mouth kicked up into a grin. "That was a favorite saying of my mother, which means that what you're counting on isn't a sure thing."

"Oh."

"Didn't your mother have a favorite saying?" he asked casually.

She closed her eyes and tried to focus on her mother's face. Suddenly, the face of a beautiful woman popped into her brain. Blonde hair and blue eyes and a friendly smile that was able to put anyone at ease. "'Don't count your chickens before they hatch.'" The words slipped out of her mouth.

"Good. What else do you remember?"

She was startled by her own revelation. Concentrating, she tried to bring more of the memory to her mind, but nothing materialized out of the mist. "Not a thing," she answered, frustration filling her voice.

"Don't worry about it."

"How can I not?" she shot back. "For all I know, I might be a criminal."

He pulled the truck to the side of the road and put the engine in park. Turning to her, he leaned against the door. "Do you remember more than you're telling me?" he asked quietly, an ominous quality to his voice.

All the blood drained from her face and she felt light-headed. "No."

"Then why would you think you might have committed a crime?" There was an edge to his words that told April she didn't want to be on the law-breaking side of this man.

"I don't know."

His gaze pierced her like a laser, cutting to the very heart of her. "Something made you say that."

April feverishly searched her memory. He was right. There was something sitting there, just beyond her consciousness, waiting like a panther to pounce once her guard was down. "You're right. There's something there, but—" Tears filled her eyes. "I don't know what it is."

He leaned forward and in his eyes she found a fountain of rest. "Relax, April. Whatever it is, it will make itself known—and when that happens, we'll deal with it together."

There was such a quiet reassurance in his words that she felt as if a great weight had been taken off her shoulders. She was safe, for now. "Thank you."

But settling back against the seat, she wondered when the panther would pounce.

As he drove, Rafe pointed out the churning waters of the small river that was now back in its banks. "What would you call the land where that stream runs?" he asked, nodding to the shallow valley.

"A riverbed?"

"No, the land around it."

She looked again at the area. "A hallow."

Rafe's eyebrow arched. "That's interesting."

"Why?"

"Because it's another clue to where you come from. A hallow is what folks around Austin call it. A draw is what people in west Texas call that land. Or in east Texas, where a lot of population is from Louisiana, they call it a gully."

"How do you know that?" she asked.

"In college, I took a course on the geography of Texas. They covered dialects within the state."

"Oh." After a moment she added, "So you think I'm from somewhere around Austin?"

"Sounds like you grew up there. You have a soft drawl that flavors your speech. From some of the ways you say things, I'd bet you're college educated and have lived in an urban area for a while."

"So we're no closer to knowing where I'm from than before." There was a note of desperation in her voice.

He couldn't harden his heart to her anxiety. He gave her a reassuring smile. "They're all pieces of the puzzle that is you. But you've come to the right man, April. Solving mysteries is my job."

Some of the tension left her eyes. "I'll count on that."

He hoped he could live up to her trust. His mind wandered back to what he'd learned from Mabel about the unidentified stranger. Something was there. Something he was going to meet head on, and it could be messy.

Rubbing the back of his neck, he tried to ease the tension knotting those muscles.

Who was the woman beside him? Where had she come from? And what was she running from? The questions kept racing through Rafe's mind. He had this 'feeling' that April was in trouble, and he never ignored his premonitions. Ten years with the Rangers had taught him that rule. His premonitions had saved his life more than once.

April's reaction to going into the sheriff's office spoke loudly of her wariness of the police. But if she had that reaction to the sheriff, why hadn't he sensed any nervousness in her when she found out that he was a Ranger? When he'd told her what he did, it hadn't seemed to bother her at all. So maybe it wasn't law enforcement that made her nervous, perhaps it was the sheriff—or the sheriff's office—that made her nervous.

Now that was interesting. Why would one law enforcement agency make her nervous, yet another not bother her? Did it have something to do with jurisdiction, or maybe just a bad experience with a sheriff.

He passed the main turn-off to his ranch and continued on. Glancing at her to see whether she recognized the road, he saw a question in her eyes.

"I'm taking the long way around to my ranch. This will bring me down County Road 4 close to where I found you. I was hoping that maybe we could come up with some evidence about your identity."

"Oh."

"You don't sound too eager."

She shrugged.

That small movement of her shoulders spoke loudly of the dilemma she was facing. April had already said she was afraid that she might be in trouble with the law. She was in trouble, all right—she had that smell to her. But he had his doubts that it was the law chasing her. Maybe it was a jealous husband—he glanced at her left hand, making sure he hadn't overlooked any ring on her finger—or a boyfriend, or a bad family situation, or a bad debt.

The road curved, skirting around his land. He slowed down, looking for signs of the flash floods. Pulling to the side of the road, he got out and walked along the edge of the blacktop. There was evidence that the water had washed over the road, taking the local plants and rocks with it. But there were no signs of a car or any clues to April's identity.

Rafe climbed back inside the cab and started the engine.

"Did you see anything?" April asked. Her teeth bit her bottom lip and her eyes filled with apprehension.

"No." He put the car in gear. "This part of the road was obviously caught in the flash flood this morning, but there are several draws around here where a car could be hidden from view. I'll need to ride around on horseback to check the area further."

She pressed her forehead against the door window. "This seems like a b-bad dream that I can't wake up from." Tears rolled down her cheeks.

"Ah, sh—" he muttered to himself. He didn't want to feel her pain and confusion. He didn't want to get involved in her problems, he was no good at this type of thing. His ex-wife let him know in no uncertain terms what a bust he'd been at meeting her needs. But looking into April's watery eyes, Rafe knew he had no choice in the matter.

Pulling the truck to the side of the road, he put it into park, then reached for her. She willingly came into his arms, and the tears she'd been holding back burst forth. Her entire body convulsed with sorrow. Rafe's hand settled on her head, his fingers tangling in her thick hair.

She clutched his shirt as if he were a life preserver and she were drowning. She raised her face to his, and it was as natural as breathing for him to settle his lips over hers. Her mouth flowered under his, welcoming the pressure.

Suddenly any idea of just offering April comfort fled his mind, as he was plunged into the passion of the kiss. She tasted of tears and honey, warmth and desire. Her arms crept around his neck and Rafe pulled her closer. Her breasts pressed into the wall of his chest and the heat burned him.

His last thread of sanity was close to snapping when he heard the harsh sound of a horn. Rafe raised his head and nearly moaned aloud when he saw April's desire for him in her rapturous expression. Hell, what kind of man took advantage of a woman who couldn't remember her own name?

Another honk cut the air, bringing Rafe's gaze to the truck coming toward them on the opposite side of the road. He set April away from him and he rolled down his window, trying to get his raging hormones under control.

"Hi, Dick," Rafe greeted his closest neighbor, trying to assume a calm demeanor. "What's going on?"

Dick glanced at the woman beside Rafe, then grinned. It was obvious he had seen what Rafe and April had been doing. "I wanted to see how you fared after this morning's storms. Did you lose any cattle?"

"Can't say. I haven't spotted any yet. Say, Dick, was your wife expecting any company this week?"

"Nope."

From Dick's expression, it was obvious the man was waiting for an explanation, or an introduction to the woman sitting next to Rafe. Rafe decided the easiest way to deal with the situation was to tell his neighbor the truth.

After introducing them, he continued, "April here was caught in a flash flood this morning. We still haven't found her car yet, so if you see one, call me."

"She all right?" Dick asked.

"She sprained her ankle, and...um...she can't remember who she is," Rafe added the last part reluctantly. "But other than that, physically she's okay. It will be easier to discover her identity when we find her missing car."

Resting his forearm on the window, Dick said, "That so? Did you take her to Dr. Alex?"

"Yup."

He looked at April, unable to disguise his curiosity. "I'll keep my eyes peeled. If I spot it, I'll give you a call."

"Thanks." Rafe waited until Dick had driven off before turning to April. The look of despair on her face made him want to reach for her and comfort her again. What was the matter with him, touching April the way he had, squeezing her hand, holding her? Carmen, his ex-wife, often complained that he didn't touch her enough and that he was a cold man.

Wisely, Rafe kept his hands wrapped over the steering wheel. Around April his perspective and good common sense evaporated. "This is only temporary, April. You've already remembered some things from your past."

Her bottom lip quivered as she nodded.

He couldn't ignore her distress. His hand covered hers. Well, hell. So much for keeping his distance. "Believe me?"

A hint of a smile played around her mouth. "Yes," she said with a spark of hope.

He released her hand. "All right. We'll get back to the ranch and start making some calls to see if anyone in the vicinity was expecting you."

"What if you don't find anyone?"

"*Mi madre* always told me not to borrow trouble, and I've always tried to do what she said."

"Somehow I don't envision you as a mama's boy."

His eyes clouded when he remembered his mother and the struggles she endured to give him the best. "I tried to make her life as good as I could."

April reached for him. When her fingers found his, her mouth turned up into an understanding smile.

His heart contracted, and somehow he knew he was in trouble here. He turned from her and put the truck into motion.

Rafe placed his paltry selection of movie tapes on the sofa next to her. "I'm sorry," he said, facing her. "All I have are war movies and Westerns."

"Don't worry. I'll find something to watch."

He studied her for a moment. "If you need anything, I'll be down the hall in my study, making those calls we talked about."

"I'll be okay." She struggled to her feet, grabbed her crutches, and awkwardly clomped toward the bathroom.

"Where are you going?" After he asked the question, he felt like a fool.

"I wanted to see if my things were dry."

"Oh."

They walked into the hall and April stepped into the bathroom. She came out a moment later, holding her jeans, shirt and shoes. "They're still damp. Do you have a clothesline or a dryer?"

He looked offended. "Do I look like a man who hangs out his laundry?"

She giggled. The sound caused the oddest reaction in him. It was like putting a match to kindling—he went up in flames.

"C'mon. I'll show you the dryer." He glanced over his shoulder at her. "I guess I should've thrown your clothes in the dryer before we left, but I was in such a hurry to get you to the doctor, it slipped my mind."

They walked back through the living room and kitchen. She paused and put her wet shoes before the refrigerator. He gave her a questioning look.

"The hot air from the refrigerator comes out there. It's the best way to dry wet shoes."

They both were struck that she'd recalled such a trivial bit of knowledge. He smiled. "See what I told you. More is coming back to you."

Although her gaze remained guarded, a smile appeared on her lips.

They walked through the kitchen to the laundry room. He opened the dryer and motioned for her to throw her things inside. Once he turned it on, they went back into the living room and she sat down.

"You need anything else?" he asked, taking her crutches and placing them by the sofa.

"I think I'll be all right."

For some unknown reason, he was loath to leave her. But he needed the privacy to talk to Derek and to go through the latest list of missing persons that the DPS had put out. He gave her a last glimpse and walked down the hall.

Once in his library, he plowed through the pile on his desk, looking for the most recent missing persons report. He found it and quickly went down the list. There was no one who resembled April. He next looked at the APB list of criminals on the run. Again, nothing. Finally, he turned on his computer and checked the FBI listing on missing persons. Nothing.

He picked up the phone and called Derek. On the third ring, Derek picked up.

"Have you found anything?" Rafe asked.

"No, but I haven't driven out to your section of the county."

"You turn up anything on that stranger at Mabel's?"

"Nope. He didn't go to any stores in town, but everyone's been warned about April and to watch for anything unusual."

Rafe knew that the folks of Saddle would be on their guard for this stranger. People pulled together in a sparsely populated county and watched out for each other.

"I'll go talk to Mabel again. Maybe she'll remember something else that could give us a clue to who this guy is."

"Thanks." Rafe hung up the phone. Running his hands through his hair, he tried to clear his head of all the extraneous thoughts and concentrate on that nagging feeling at the edge of his mind.

He tried to bring his anxiety into focus, but after about five minutes, he gave up. There just wasn't enough information.

Over the next ten minutes, Rafe called all his closest neighbors and asked them if any had been expecting a visitor. No one had.

Then he went back over the lists again to make sure he hadn't overlooked something. But he found nothing new.

Maybe what was bothering him was the attraction he felt for April. With is ex-wife, there had been sizzle in the beginning. But after a while, the zing had seemed to leave the marriage, and work had held more interest for him than going home to hear his wife list his shortcomings. And she had done that numerous times.

The other thing that had caught Rafe off guard was that April was a beautiful blond-haired, green-eyed woman. He was from a mixed heritage, neither all Anglo nor all Hispanic. As a youth, he had wanted to belong, and since his mother had been Hispanic, he thought his perfect mate would be Hispanic. Obviously, that hadn't worked. Now he was gun-shy and unwilling to risk his heart.

Quit hiding, a voice in his head scolded him. *Go out and face her.*

Taking a deep breath, he stood and walked down the hall. Pausing at the door, he heard a voice singing, "Just you wait, Henry Higgins, just you wait."

He smiled. *My Fair Lady* had been his mother's favorite movie. He'd forgotten that he'd kept her copy of it.

"Are you enjoying the movie?" he asked as he walked into the room. April was resting on the couch, her ankle up on the coffee table. He sat down beside her.

She grinned. "Somehow you don't look like the kind of guy who likes musicals."

"I don't. That copy was my mother's. I kept it after she died."

April's smile faded. "Oh, I'm sorry."

He looked at the screen. "Mom always liked the Cinderella aspect of this movie. I guess she identified with the heroine." Feeling awkward, he added, "Why don't I go get that surprise Mabel sent us? Two pieces of Red Velvet cake."

"I could get very spoiled here and not want to go home." When April realized what she'd said, all color drained from her face.

Standing, Rafe smiled at her. "I don't think there's a chance of that."

He walked into the kitchen and set up the coffee-maker, then unwrapped the pieces of cake. Walking back into the room, he handed her a plate, then set the other one on the coffee table. "You have your choice of coffee or a soft drink. What would you like?"

"Is your coffee half as good as it smells?"

"Are you kidding? Rangers are known to make the best coffee in west Texas—next to Mabel's, that is."

"Coffee, please."

He nodded, walked back into the kitchen and poured two cups of coffee. "You like it black or diluted with cream and sugar?" he asked.

"Diluted. Cream only," she answered back.

He fished out the coffee creamer and stirred in a big spoonful. "You're making progress, April," he called out. "Remembering how you like your coffee is a step forward."

She was smiling when he came back into the room. "It is."

"Your guard was down, and your preference slipped out. It's a good sign."

They ate in companionable silence and watched the movie. Rafe's feelings grew more raw as the movie progressed. Seeing it made him relive the last time he'd watched it with his mother.

"Would you tell me about your mom?" April whispered when the movie ended.

The request surprised him, and at first he didn't want to talk about it. Then he noticed the longing in her eyes. It occurred to him that April at this moment didn't have a past of her own, so it was natural that she wanted something to fill that void.

"What can I say? Since you met my half sister, it's obvious that my mother wasn't with my dad for long. They were young, in love, and not married." He shook his head, wondering how that brief, intense time could've lasted her a lifetime. "Before my mom could tell my dad she was pregnant, he'd left the Valley and gone to Midland to see if he could make money in the oil fields there. He was a wildcatter and on his first well he was running out of money. So when the daughter of a local banker became interested in him, he married her and obtained the loan he needed to strike it big with his well."

April reached out and touched his hand. He tried to smile at her, but the memories kept pulling him back into the bitterness of the past.

"Why didn't your mom try to contact your dad?"

He shrugged. "In her things, I found the announcement for George's first marriage. Obviously, Mother knew about his marriage. George later told me that he saw Mom a couple of years after he married the first time. My guess is that George came looking for sympathy from his old flame and maybe something more.

But he didn't get it. My mother wasn't going to allow him back into her life. And she didn't tell him about me.

"Mom was shunned by her family for having a baby out of wedlock. It shamed them. I don't think the situation would've been so bad if it hadn't been obvious that I was half Anglo. A mistake could be forgiven, but what she did was an anathema."

Rafe stood up and walked to the bank of windows that overlooked his front yard. "But my mother was a determined woman. Her aunt never turned her back on her, and helped mom through court reporting school. Mom graduated first in her class and found a job right away. She worked herself into a top position within the county courts. Unfortunately, she never reconciled with her parents. Her brothers and sisters eventually invited her to family functions, but her father never spoke to her again for causing the family shame."

Running his hand through his hair, he turned and faced April. From her expression, it was obvious that she felt the emotions the story had caused him. But he wanted her to know the one bright point in the story.

"When I became a Ranger, my mother said if she had it all to do over again, she'd do it again in a heartbeat. She'd loved my dad, and I was…the joy of her life." Suddenly, he was chagrined that he had let that last bit of information slip.

When he looked into April's eyes, there were tears there. And understanding—a sentiment that his ex-wife had never given him.

"Thank you for telling me."

He was in dangerous, uncharted waters here. He needed to get away. "I'd better go out and finish riding the last section of land to see if I have any cows caught in the flash flood. I also need to keep an eye out for your car. Why don't you watch another tape. I shouldn't be more than a couple of hours."

"Okay." She sounded lost and alone.

He cursed silently, but knew he needed to get out there.

As he rode from the house, he had the oddest feeling that he was running away from something—something he didn't want to face.

Chapter 4

April went through Rafe's videotapes once more. She wasn't in the mood for a war movie. Somehow death and destruction didn't appeal to her at the moment. She switched off the VCR and silence descended, wrapping around her, leaving her feeling lost and alone. Who was she and where had she come from?

No answers appeared.

Instead of facing those stark, unanswered questions, April glanced around the neat room, trying to concentrate on Rafe. For a single man living by himself, he seemed very neat. Nothing was out of place. The furniture was dusty, but the house seemed orderly—which, oddly enough, set her teeth on edge. Rafe's clothes and boots weren't lying around. There weren't any dirty dishes on the end tables or even in the kitchen sink. And that made April uneasy.

Her curiosity driving her, April walked down the hall and stopped in the open doorway of Rafe's office. The room was excessively neat. Nothing was out of place in the well-used room. Papers were neatly stacked in the trays on his desk. There was even a stack of papers on the blotter, but they were lined up and neat.

A shiver passed over her skin.

She hobbled further down the hall. At the end was a large bedroom with massive pieces of furniture. She peeked inside. Again, orderly. There was nothing out of place. There were no clothes or shoes scattered across the floor. Again, his neatness made her restless, but she didn't understand why.

Turning, she walked back into the living room. The quiet of the room pressed down on her, increasing her nervousness. She walked over to the window and looked out at the distant mountains.

How had she ended up on Rafe's land? That was a question that held both a promise and a threat.

Not wanting to think about it anymore, she moved into the kitchen. She needed to do something—an activity that would take her mind off her unsolved questions. She decided to make dinner. Opening the refrigerator, she saw a package of chili meat. She opened several cabinets and was amazed at the unorganized way that Rafe had put his dishes and canned goods on the shelves. It was a disaster—there was no organized pattern to the contents and April found comfort in the disorganization.

Rafe was human, after all. A smile tickled her lips.

She searched several cabinets until she found cans of green chilies and pinto beans. Pulling out a frying pan, she began to fry the meat. Maybe if she kept herself busy making dinner, she wouldn't worry about her situation.

She could only pray.

* * *

Rafe surveyed the area where he had found April. There were fresh signs of the flash flood, but if the water had washed her car away, he couldn't find any sign of it.

He took a deep breath, inhaling the sweet smell of washed earth. He needed to concentrate on what to do next, instead of remembering how lost and alone April had looked when he walked out the back door. But he'd had no choice in the matter, he kept telling himself.

Suddenly, his horse's head came up and the ears came forward.

"What is it Sam?" Rafe asked.

The sound of an engine pierced the air. Rafe looked down the county road and saw the sheriff's car come to a stop. Derek climbed out.

"How's it going, Rafe?" Derek asked.

"This is where I found April. But I don't see any signs of her car. Have you spotted it?"

Derek shook his head. "No. Of course there are hundreds of places it could be out here."

"I'll call in the highway patrol helicopters to search this area. I'll contact them when I get back to the ranch. Did you check on the wanted list for someone resembling April?"

"There was nothing on the state. Nothing on the national, either."

Rafe rubbed the back of his neck, trying to put his finger on the sense of disquiet hammering him. "We'll need to keep a close watch on the missing persons list. It's early, yet." He was making up excuses. "I expect within the next twelve hours someone will report her missing."

"Did you call your neighbors?"

"Sure did. No one was expecting a guest." He rolled his shoulders, trying to work out the knot in his neck.

"What's bothering you, Rafe?"

Shaking his head, Rafe said, "Am I that obvious?"

"Only to those of us who know you."

"That gut feeling about trouble following April is still there. I don't know how or what, but something's going to show up."

"Well, all we can do is watch and wait."

"And that's what frustrates me the most. Feeling something's out of kilter, and not knowing what it is."

"Look at it this way, Rafe. The best lawmen have that sixth sense. You're in a select group."

"And you're telling me you didn't know when Alex was in trouble at Simon Moore's ranch?" Rafe said, referring to the time his sister was in danger from a major drug dealer.

"Hey, we all get them. I'll trust your instincts on this one, Rafe." He got back into his cruiser and drove off.

Rafe mounted his horse and started back to the ranch. By the time he approached the ranch house, he'd managed to pull one cow out of a mud hole and return a lost calf to the main herd and its anxious mother. But his added mission—to find a clue to April's identity—had been a complete wash. And his talk with Derek hadn't led to any new information.

Dismounting, he hurriedly took care of his horse and strode to the house. The smell that greeted him when he opened the door shocked him, hurtling him back over the years to when his mother cooked for him.

Chili.

A shaft of loneliness pierced Rafe's heart, but he refused to give in to the feelings. Another odd and equally shattering thought popped into his head—a wife, preparing dinner for her husband.

He stopped that idea cold. No sir. He'd traveled that road before, and he hadn't fared well.

Hanging his hat by the back door, he was drawn by the smell of honest-to-goodness green chili—not the stuff out of a can—to the stove.

Glancing over her shoulder, April gave him a full smile that sent a jolt of electricity through his body, pooling in the part of his anatomy that had been unruly since April appeared this morning. It had nothing to do with food, but everything to do with hunger. Her crutches were resting on the counter next to her.

"What are you doing?" His voice sounded rough as he struggled with his desires.

April's smile faded and her eyes grew haunted. "Cooking."

Rafe felt two inches tall. It wasn't April's fault that he found her attractive. She'd done nothing but be herself. "What I meant was, why are you up on your feet?"

The question didn't ease the worry in her eyes. "I needed something to do besides wondering who I was."

"Didn't you want to watch a movie?"

"I didn't want to see any war movies. They tend not to brighten a person's mood."

He couldn't blame her. "It smells delicious," he commented, trying to ease her strained expression.

"You like chili?" she asked softly.

He grinned. "Does a Texan brag? Of course I love it." He peered over her shoulder at the frying pan.

Seeing the direction of his gaze, she said, "I saw the meat in the refrigerator, and I thought—" she shrugged her shoulders "—you might like some homemade chili."

He cocked his head. "You're a mind reader. I like my chili cooked from scratch with green chilies. It reminds me of the way my mother made it. How did you learn to do that?"

Her gaze flew to his. Surprise colored her green eyes—eyes the color of the first grass of spring. Irritated with himself, Rafe turned toward the cabinets to get a coffee cup.

"I don't know. I just started cooking to keep myself busy." She gave him a wobbly smile. "Your selection of tapes was rather...uh...limited."

"Hey, I'm a bachelor. What did you expect?"

She shrugged.

"If that chili tastes half as good as it smells, I'm in for a real treat. Not many people make it from scratch that way. Most folks cook the mild red stuff, or open a can. How did you learn to make it?" he asked again, hoping that if she remembered how to cook, maybe she'd remember how she *learned* to cook.

"I—" She looked down at the pan and her brow wrinkled. "I don't know."

"Don't worry. I'm thankful you made it. You'd think I'd learn to cook just out of self-defense."

"Then why'd you have that chili meat in your refrigerator if you don't cook?"

How could he explain the yearning that had possessed him to buy that meat. "I had a hankering."

"You don't look like you're starving." Her gaze moved slowly over his body and he felt each tense muscle as her eyes caressed him. It was becoming increasingly clear that he was headed for trouble if he couldn't keep his mind on solving the mystery of April's identity. Maybe he needed to call one of his neighbors.

"I eat at Mabel's a lot." He turned to the bread box and pulled out a bag of tortillas.

"In addition to the pinto beans, I made a couple of salads." She nodded toward the refrigerator. "They're in there."

"I'm surprised that the lettuce was still good," he said, laughing. He took the bowls out and set them on the table. Rafe finished setting the table, adding a couple of cans of soda to the mix. He then carried the skillet to the table, April hobbling after him.

Rafe dished out the chili, then tore off a couple of pieces of tortilla and scooped up a piece of meat. The spicy flavor brought back a dozen different memories.

"How is it?" she asked.

"You've got a talent there, April. I think you could give Mabel some competition."

She smiled gratefully, then tasted her creation. "It's not bad.

"Did you find any signs of my car?" she asked, spearing a tomato.

"Nope. I checked the area where I found you. There wasn't anything. Derek drove by and he hadn't found anything, either. But there are a lot of *arroyos* in the area—places where we wouldn't notice a car. I'll call the DPS office in Marfa and see if I can get one of the surveillance helicopters to fly over this area. They can cover more ground than I can on horseback. If they spot something, then we can go out and get the tag number and identify you that way."

"Oh." She couldn't help the note of desolation in her voice. Why couldn't the answers be easier?

He smiled warmly, making her pulse speed up.

"You're worrying too much. Don't push it."

She looked down at her hands, and it felt like she'd

swallowed a dozen butterflies. When her gaze lifted again, it locked with Rafe's, and those butterflies went wild. She should be frightened of being alone with this stranger. What did she know of him? All she knew was that he was a Texas Ranger. And that he was neat.

"I was impressed by how neat you keep your house," April said.

Surprise crossed his face. "My mother worked. It made her life easier if I picked up after myself." He shrugged. "I guess I just never got out of the habit."

And with those words, her discomfort with his neatness slipped away. She stood and picked up her plate.

"What are you doing?" he asked.

"I'm gathering the dishes."

"Since you cooked, I'll clean. Besides, you've been up on that foot too long. You go rest."

If he'd said he wanted to have sex with her, here in the middle of the kitchen, she couldn't have been more surprised.

"Ah—"

"Close your mouth, April. My offer isn't so surprising, especially in this day and age."

He was right. Surprisingly enough, she understood about the changing role of men and women today. If she remembered that unimportant data, why couldn't she remember who she was?

"Why don't you go turn on the TV? The local news should be coming on."

"Local?" Her brow wrinkled in a frown. Surely he didn't mean Saddle.

"Midland," he supplied. "They might have something about you. It's a chance."

She moved slowly to the television and turned it on. As she watched the commentator on the screen, she heard Rafe in the kitchen. When the newscast moved into the weather for tomorrow, April didn't know whether to feel relieved that news of an escaped convict—her—hadn't been there, or disappointed that no one had missed her enough to report her gone.

It had only been hours since Rafe had found her, but it felt like a lifetime.

"Well, I guess we'll have to approach this problem from a different angle," Rafe said, sitting down next to April.

"How?" She couldn't keep the frustration out of her voice.

"April, you are not the first missing person that I've tracked down."

"But I don't even know—"

He rested his finger across her lips, stopping her words. But his touch set off sparks of another kind that had been smoldering in her. The fire seemed to blaze out of control. Apparently, he felt it too, because he drew his hand back.

Clearing his throat, he said, "Don't worry about your memory. You're alive. Often, I've tracked people down who couldn't tell me who they were because they weren't in the land of the living."

If he had the answers, she thought, maybe he could share them with her. "So what are we going to do?"

His eyes sparked with humor. "Don't believe me, huh?"

He'd pegged her, she realized. "What can I say?"

"Tomorrow, we'll drive to Alpine and go to the newspaper and have them run a story on the lovely lady without a memory." His description warmed her. "You'll be big news in this area of the state. If you're from around here, or maybe supposed to be visiting friends, we'll discover it.''

"And if I'm not?" She couldn't help the negative thoughts rumbling around in her head.

"We still haven't got back the report from the state on your fingerprints. Remember, not only criminals are listed in that computer. State employees are there, too. With your worn-down fingerprints, it would make sense that you worked for the state, doing some sort of paperwork.''

"Yes, but—"

"And there's the FBI database. And a database of fingerprints for stockbrokers. And then—"

She raised her hands. "Okay, okay, I surrender. I'll think positive thoughts.''

"I'll hold you to your word.''

From the tone of his voice, it was obvious to April that lying to Rafe wasn't an option.

Rafe turned off the television as soon as the ten o'clock news was over. April's eyes were heavy.

"Why don't you do what you need to do in the bathroom, and I'll get you one of my T-shirts to sleep in.''

"Also, could you get my clothes out of the dryer so I'll have something else to wear tomorrow besides these scrubs?''

He helped her stand and gave her the crutches. Once she was safely in the bathroom, he went into his bedroom and got a T-shirt, then went to the washroom to retrieve her clothes. He placed everything on the bed in the second bedroom. He heard the bathroom door open, then stepped out into the hall. April glanced at him.

In spite of the situation, Rafe found himself being sucked down into this vortex of emotion. He had no right to feel anything for this woman except compassion. Yet somehow, his body's reaction wasn't out of kindness.

"I left the things on the bed," he said, stating the obvious.

"Thank you." She hobbled toward the door. When she got even with him, her eyes met his with electrifying results. Her gaze slid away from his and she silently went into the room and closed the door.

That kiss he'd shared with April this afternoon had been a major, Texas-sized mistake. He could still remember the taste of her mouth, the feel of her skin, the softness of her body pressed against his.

Rafe realized with blinding, heart-stopping clarity that this was going to be one of those cases that either makes or breaks a man.

He turned and headed to the library. He needed to call the highway patrol and line up the DPS helicopter to search this area for April's car. They might get lucky. He hoped so.

April slipped into Rafe's shirt and her face turned crimson with the reaction of her body. Her nipples hardened and her mouth went dry.

"You're acting like a goose," she mumbled to herself. "The man doesn't—" She swallowed the rest of the lie. It was obvious that Rafe felt the sparks that seemed to leap from her to him. But he hadn't acted on them since the kiss, much to her relief.

Pulling back the bedspread, she awkwardly got under the covers. As soon as she found a comfortable spot on her side, thoughts of Rafe came back to her. He was a handsome man with black hair and deep brown eyes that could focus with such intensity that it was like a spotlight, cutting through the darkness.

She closed her eyes and tried to clear her mind. But she couldn't help recalling that each time he'd carried her to his truck, she'd felt the rock hard muscles of his arms and chest. Instead of relaxing, the feelings of sitting in front of Rafe on his horse as they rode back from where he found her exploded into her brain. She might have been woozy then, but apparently her mind had registered every detail of the incident, because it was replaying now with stunning clarity.

What was wrong with her to be thinking about Rafe when she didn't even know her own name? What if she had a husband? And children?

She stared at her empty left hand.

Obviously, what she was feeling was just gratitude to Rafe for helping her, nothing else.

Yeah, and do you still believe in the Easter Bunny? a voice in her head whispered.

Well, she couldn't do anything about the attraction she felt, but she could do something about acting on that attraction. She wouldn't. Then when she discovered who she was, she wouldn't feel guilty. It was the best she could do.

Rafe felt as if he'd spent the night wrestling an alligator. His muscles were tense and sore, and there was no feeling of renewal when he'd woken. In fact, he felt worse this morning than he had last night when he went to bed.

What had become crystal clear to him in those dark hours was that he had no business feeling anything for April except the concern a peace officer would have for a victim. And he was going to stick to that resolve.

He went into the kitchen and began making coffee.

As the smell floated through the room, he cracked open several eggs into a bowl.

"Good mornin'."

April's soft voice went straight to his heart. "Morning."

It appeared from the lines of fatigue under her eyes that April hadn't rested well, either. The wall he'd been trying to erect took a major hit.

"Can I help?" she asked.

"Naw. I can do a fairly decent job scrambling eggs. But I think the coffee's done if you want to pour us a cup."

Her face broke into a smile. "Where do you keep your cups?"

He indicated the cabinet in the corner of the kitchen. She limped to where he pointed.

"Are you sure you still shouldn't be on those crutches?" he asked.

"My ankle's feeling much better this morning." After retrieving the cups, she poured them coffee. "I'm looking forward to going into Alpine today. I'm hoping the story will give us clues as to who I am."

Rafe pulled out two plates and dished out the eggs.

"Even if we don't have any calls, at least we'll know more about you—even if it is a negative." He set the plates on the table, then sat down and gave her a reassuring smile. "You're alive and healthy. The rest of it is gravy."

"I like the way you think, Rafe."

He just wished he felt as positive as he sounded.

April flinched as the camera's flash went off. "Sorry," she told the photographer.

"Don't worry," the man told her. "I'll just keep snapping while you finish your interview with Scott. I'll get some good shots.''

April stared down at her wrinkled shirt and jeans. She looked like a beggar, she thought.

''So you remember who the president is, but you don't remember your own name or anything about yourself before Rafe found you? Is that right?'' The young reporter was eager, bright and interested in April's story.

''That's right.''

''Well, we'll run this in the paper tomorrow, so if anyone knows you, you should get some sort of result on Saturday.''

''And you'll put into the story that if anyone knows anything to call either the sheriff's office or my office number,'' Rafe added.

Scott smiled. ''I will, Ranger Sanchez.''

Rafe knew he was being extra cautious, but he felt it was important that April hear how they dealt with this situation. ''Thanks for everything, Scott. Say hi to your dad for me.''

Although April's ankle felt better today, she still couldn't put on her shoe, so she had opted to use her crutches. She hobbled out to Rafe's truck, and he helped her inside.

''Let's stop by the sheriff's office and see if they have turned up anything on you.''

She shrugged. But as Rafe drove the few blocks, he kept his eyes on April, wanting to gauge her reaction to going to the sheriff's office. She seemed to tense up as she had the day before at Derek's office. Her teeth chewed her bottom lip.

The warning bells went off in Rafe's head.

It appeared that sheriffs bothered April. Rangers, no. But sheriffs, yes. It would be interesting to see her reaction to the police, but since Alpine's sheriff's office and police were one and the same, he guessed he wouldn't get the opportunity.

The instant they entered the office, Rafe spotted Wesley Clayton, the sheriff, sitting on the edge of one of the desks. He was a tall man with silver hair and a salt-and-pepper mustache.

"What brings you to town, Rafe?" Wesley asked as he stood.

Rafe eased April forward. "I have a lady here, Wes, who doesn't know her identity. I found her on my property yesterday afternoon. I thought I'd check all your APB's and let her meet you, so if someone comes looking for her, you'll know where to find her. We've already done an article for the paper, hoping someone will recognize her."

It took nearly forty-five minutes for them to review all the missing persons lists and check with the state to see if they finished running April's prints. They hadn't.

"If anything turns up, Rafe, we'll let you know."

"I know you will, Wes. Will I see you tomorrow at Dick's get together?" Rafe asked.

"You know I wouldn't miss one of Dick's parties. He serves the best barbecue in this part of the state. Besides, his wife, Maria, makes the best chili I've tasted in a long time."

"You haven't tasted April's chili. I believe she could run a close second to Maria."

Wes's gaze zeroed in on April. "Really?"

April gave the sheriff a weak smile. "I may not know who I am, but apparently I know how to fix green chili. How I don't know, but...." She looked down at her feet.

"Have you taken April to the hospital here in town?" Wes asked.

"Not yet. Dr. Alex examined her and didn't find anything wrong. But I thought we'd stop by the hospital before we leave and have her checked out."

"Well, I'll keep my ears open—see if anyone mentions anything about the story, or missing a friend or relative."

"Thanks, Wes."

As they left the building, it was as if a weight had been taken off her shoulders. April's entire demeanor seemed to lighten. And Rafe knew he had a lead that he needed to follow. April was nervous around sheriffs.

They drove to the hospital and saw one of the doctors that had attended Rafe the last time he'd been shot. Dr. Evans assured Rafe that his sister's original assessment seemed right on the mark.

"If she doesn't have some inkling of who she is in a week's time, bring her back and we'll do some more testing. But I think, with time, everything should clear up for her."

Rafe looked at April. "Is there anything else we can do?"

The doctor looked at April, then Rafe. "Try praying."

Rafe sat up in his chair. "Is that your medical opinion?"

"No. I gave you my medical opinion. Apparently, you didn't like it, so I offered another suggestion."

"Don't give up your day job, doc, you're a better doctor than you are a comedian."

"April's situation needs time, Rafe. That's the best thing for the time being."

"Okay, okay, I get the picture."

As they were walking out to his truck, April began to laugh. "Are you friends with Dr. Evans?"

"I thought I was. Apparently—"

"He thinks you're an impatient man. Now, why would he think that?"

Rafe felt himself blush. He remembered clearly the fight that Marvin Evans and he had had over his recuperation the last time he was shot. Marv thought he needed more time off. Rafe hadn't listened, and regretted ignoring the doctor's warning. This time, he would heed the man's advice. "Let's just say I've learned the hard way to pay attention to Marv."

Rafe studied the wrinkled jeans and shirt that April wore. He didn't have much back at his house for her to wear. Since they were here in Alpine, he might as well get her some clothes. When they stopped in front of the department store, April gave him a puzzled look.

"What are we doing here?"

"We don't know how long it will take for your memory to return. And you can't go around in what you have on. So we're going to get some things for you."

Surprise filled her eyes. "I don't have any money—"

"Don't worry about it, April."

"But—"

He slid out of the truck and closed the door. It appeared his lost lady was going to put up a fight. Opening the passenger door, he waited for her to hand him the crutches. It took several minutes to get her inside the building.

"Rafe, what are you doing here?" a gray-haired woman asked as she came from behind the desk at the back of the store.

"Katie, I've got a lady who's managed to lose her memory. She'll be staying with me a few days, but she's going to need some things. Can you help her?"

Folding her hand over her chest, Katie replied, "I

think I can. She'll need some jeans, shirts, underwear, shoes." She looked at Rafe. "Anything else?"

"Yeah. We're going to Dick's party Saturday night. I think April might need something for that."

"I don't think—" April began.

Katie laid her hand on April's arm. "Don't worry, honey. I've got the perfect dress for that."

"But—"

"Honey, my momma told me never to look a gift horse in the mouth."

April sent Rafe a wary glance. "But wouldn't Rafe want to know the price of what you're going to show me?"

"Rafe? Naw, he's a good man. Fair, too. He won't care. Will you, Rafe?" Katie asked him.

"I'll trust your judgment, Katie."

"I knew there was a reason I liked you."

He heard Katie's laugh as she escorted April to the rear of the store.

Forty-five minutes later, April stood in front of the mirror in the dressing room, looking at the yards of lavender gauze in the skirt of the sleeveless dress. A hot-pink belt was the focal point.

"Oh, you look like a vision in that," Katie said, smiling at April. "Why don't you show Rafe?"

April's gaze shifted from the mirror to Katie. Her delight in the dress turned into nervousness at the thought of showing this to Rafe. But why?

"C'mon. Rafe will be swept off his feet when he sees you." There was a cat-ate-the-canary grin on Katie's face as she grabbed April's arm and pulled her out of the dressing room. April's gait was awkward because of her hurt ankle. She felt like a fish flopping on the shore.

"Rafe, come look at this," Katie called out.

Rafe, who had been staring out the window, turned and locked his gaze onto April. Slowly his eyes wandered over her form—from her face, over her breasts, hips, then down to her feet, one bare and the other in a tennis shoe. His gaze touched off a fire in her blood.

"The shoe doesn't match," he muttered absently.

"Is that all you can say, Ranger Sanchez?" Katie's voice held an indignant tone.

A slow, sensuous smile curved his mouth. "No." He turned to Katie. "But I don't believe you'd want me to say what I'm thinkin'."

The older woman gave a satisfied grin. "I see. Well, if that's your reaction, then I'd say April should take the dress."

Rafe's gaze met April's. The amusement fled from his eyes, replaced by burning heat. "You look *muy hermosa.*" He said it so quietly, so softly that it went straight to her heart and exploded with sizzle and color.

"She'll knock them dead at Dick's shindig on Saturday night."

"That, she will." There was a quiet certainty in his voice and his eyes never left her.

Her blood raced through her body.

"She'll be the talk of the county for weeks."

"That's why I want to take her to the party. We need to find out if anyone knows anything about her."

April felt a curious sense of disappointment at his remark. It made sense. They needed to know who she was. But...

But what, you ninny? a voice in her head challenged. *He's a Ranger. It's his job to help you. It's nothing personal.*

"She might need some shoes to wear on Saturday

night," Rafe pointed out.

"Oh," Katie gasped, looking at April's feet. "You're right. Flats, I'd say, with her ankle bad like it is." Katie disappeared down one of the aisles of the store.

April approached Rafe. "Are you sure you want me to get this?" she asked in a whisper. She glanced down at the price tag hanging from under her arm. "I mean—with everything—it's too much."

His eyebrow arched. "The men you'll see at the party will line up to take turns dancing with you—that is, if your ankle is in good enough shape by Saturday night."

"But—"

"Here's some crocheted flats," Katie interrupted, "that should work with that dress, and be easy on that swollen ankle." Katie looked at Rafe to give him the opportunity to refuse to buy the items.

Instead he said, "Box it all up, Katie, and send me the bill."

Katie grinned. "You always had good taste, Rafe."

He looked squarely at April. "I know."

April knew he wasn't talking about clothes.

Chapter 5

As April changed back into her jeans and shirt, Rafe wondered about her reaction to the shopping trip. When she'd put on the first skirt and blouse, she'd come out of the dressing room with a tentative look in her eye, as if she was worried that he would object to the simple clothes. But they looked good to him, so good that he wanted to do more than just see them.

He'd reined in his wayward thoughts, remembering that they had yet to get April's fingerprints back from the state. Perhaps she was wanted for some crime.

As April had tried on more things, her mood seemed to lighten, like a kid who had just discovered mom was going to let her have candy. She delighted in each of the outfits that Katie had brought out. Her reaction led Rafe to wonder if her response was from previous experience. Had someone in her past denied her pretty things?

When she had emerged in the lavender dress, Rafe thought the bottom of his stomach had somehow dropped out. His response to her showed him that he was going to have to be careful. April was managing to tap into a part of his emotions that was basic, and, it appeared, unwilling to be controlled.

"Do you want anything else, Rafe?" Katie's voice drew him out of his thoughts. When he looked up, he saw April hovering near the cash register in the wrinkled things she'd worn into the store. There was a look of anxiety in her big green eyes.

She was an emotional powder keg, ready to shatter his peaceful world. After the last year and a half of family trauma that he'd endured—from his mom dying to discovering his father and three sisters—his life had finally settled down. Or so he'd thought.

"Rafe?"

Again, Katie's voice brought him back to the here and now. He gave the woman a smile. "No."

April gave him a worried look. "You don't have to do this. I'm a stranger."

"Don't worry, April. I can afford it."

Oddly enough, after all the years of struggling, making do on a Ranger's salary, his life had turned around with his inheritance of the ranch, and his finding out his dad was a multimillionaire. Besides, watching the excitement and joy in April's eyes was worth every penny he spent.

Oh, you've got it bad. The thought popped into his head, but Rafe chose to ignore it. Instead he comforted himself with the idea that someone needed to help April, and who better than the Ranger assigned to this area of Texas. It was his job.

Oh sure. The thought mocked him.

Rafe pulled his truck to a stop in the parking lot of the local grocery store. He smiled at April, who was looking around, surprised at their destination.

"You saw the condition of my refrigerator and pantry. I have nothing to eat, so I thought we'd stop and shop." He reached behind the seat, pulled out the crocheted shoes from the bag, and handed them to April. "You might want to wear these instead of using those crutches."

She took the shoes and quickly changed. After helping her out of the cab of his truck, they went inside.

"Hey, Rafe, whatcha doing?" an older man called out from the counter at the front of the store.

"Ray, come meet a pretty lady that I'm taking care of." Rafe pulled April to his side. He planned to let everyone in the store know about April. The more folks who knew, the better.

The older man came down from his desk and shook April's hand as Rafe introduced them.

"April here has lost her memory. Got any idea who she might be?" Rafe asked.

"No," Ray replied. "I haven't heard anything about a missing lady."

"You will. It will be in tomorrow's paper. If anyone knows anything, just have them call me."

"Sure enough, Rafe. Sorry, Miss, about your memory."

As they went through the store, Rafe did most of the shopping. But he kept asking April if she had any preferences. The only thing that it appeared she wanted was chocolate. Pudding. Ice cream. Cookies. When she reached for brownie mix, he couldn't help but laugh. She jumped.

"Is this okay?" she asked, her voice tentative.

"I'm sorry I laughed. But it appears you have a

'thing' for chocolate.'' He looked pointedly at the items in the shopping cart.

She stared at the items. Her lips twitched, then she giggled. "I guess I do." She grabbed the brownie mix. "I can put this back."

Rafe's hand shot out, stopping her movement. "Don't. I find I have a weakness—" his eyes roamed over her face and he felt the attraction that pulled him to April surge "—for chocolate, too."

"Are you sure?"

Although he knew she meant about the brownies, his answer had nothing to do with chocolate. "Oh, yes, I'm sure."

As they drove back to Saddle, April watched the scenery carefully, praying that something would jog her memory. Nothing so far had.

"Don't worry, April. The odds are with you that your memory will return."

Surprise widened her eyes as she turned to Rafe. "How did you know that's what I was thinking about?"

"I'm a Ranger. It's my job to know." There was a light note in his voice, as if he were teasing her.

"So, you're telling me Rangers are psychic? It explains a lot of the Ranger history."

He went still. "And what would that be?"

"Oh, when Captain McNelly went into Mexico—" April stopped abruptly, then turned and stared at Rafe. "I remember the story of how McNelly and a few Rangers chased cattle rustlers in Mexico, and against overwhelming odds captured the rustlers and returned the cattle. But how can I remember something so specific when I don't know where I live?"

"Do you remember anything else about the Rangers besides that incident?" he asked her.

April closed her eyes and took a deep breath, trying to still her racing heart. She recalled several other stories of famous exploits that the Rangers had engaged in over the hundred-and-fifty-year existence of the organization. She told them to Rafe.

"Now why do you suppose that I can tell you stories of frontier justice but can't recall where I grew up?"

He shrugged his shoulders. "I'll call Alex and the doc we just saw. They might be able to shed some light on the matter."

As they drove through the countryside, April wondered why she had remembered so unique an incident. Did it mean anything? "Do you suppose my remembering about Rangers has something to do with you finding me near your house?"

Rafe's brow furrowed. "Yeah, I think you might be onto something there."

"That might explain why I was out there on that road. Where is the next closest Ranger stationed?"

"El Paso and Midland."

"Then I might have been going to see *you?*" Excitement throbbed in her voice.

"Could be." He didn't share her enthusiasm, she noted. But why? As soon as the thought occurred to her, April felt the blood drain from her face. "Maybe I did something...."

"I don't think so."

Her startled gaze flew to his face. "Why do you say that?" She couldn't keep the note of hope out of her voice.

"Look at it logically, April. If you were running from the Rangers, why would you be coming to me? And why would you remember Ranger history when you can't even tell me what you ate the day before yesterday?''

She shrugged.

"I think there's another reason. Perhaps you needed the Rangers's help.''

That thought hadn't occurred to her. All she had been going on was emotion. With Rafe she felt safe. With the sheriff, yesterday and today, she was edgy.

"Do you know what Rangers do?'' he asked gently.

The question stumped her. "Not really. But that doesn't make any sense. How could I remember those stories and not know what modern Rangers do?''

"Amnesia's a funny thing. Now, what modern Rangers do is serve as crime scene investigators for smaller police departments. Our lab serves all the counties of the state. And in both east Texas and in west Texas, we do the lion's share of the work.

"And the other thing Rangers do is police the police. We investigate corruption in local police or sheriff's departments. We're the guys that put the fear of—well, sometimes we're not liked.''

"Oh.''

"What does that mean?''

"Well, I guess I was expecting—''

"The age of the Ranger as a maverick is gone. Of course, there are some of us who still believe in that old saying, 'One Ranger, one riot.''' He grinned at her.

April felt herself drawn to Rafe in spite of the fact that she shouldn't be. Her heart was torn and ragged, and Rafe's smile seemed to be the salve that eased the hurt.

When Rafe pulled his pickup into the driveway of his ranch, he came around and helped April into the house.

It took several trips to get all the groceries and clothing inside.

She began to unpack the food, setting it on the counter. "Where does all this go?" she asked Rafe.

He paused. "Anywhere you want to put it. The pantry, or that cabinet there." He pointed to the cabinet in the corner of the kitchen. "I'm not particular."

April couldn't quite believe her ears. Put it anywhere? Didn't that sound just like a man? "You don't keep your office that way," she mumbled as she carried several cans to the pantry.

"You better know I keep things in order there. Every piece of paper is important." His tone was forceful, catching her off guard.

"Then why keep your kitchen this way?" she asked.

"Because I don't give a rat's a—whisker what my kitchen looks like."

Realizing how she was challenging him, a dark cloud seemed to pass over her heart, chilling her.

Rafe noticed her response.

"You okay?" he asked.

There was no anger in his voice and it eased her fears.

She shook off that grimness. "You need someone to take care of you," she said, trying to recapture their earlier lightness.

He paused and stared at her. "I've been down that road. It wasn't worth the price I had to pay."

His stark tone startled her so much that every thought flew out of her head, and that somber cloud returned with a vengeance. An icy finger of fear slid down her spine. "I—I didn't mean to pry."

He shrugged. "Don't worry."

But she couldn't help but worry. Folding the paper sacks, she wondered if his attitude would change toward her. If he settled into a bad mood, would she have to tiptoe around him? Would he pout or maybe use violence?

She stopped, her hand resting on a can of tomatoes she'd just shelved. Where had that thought come from? Rafe hadn't shown any tendency toward violence, so far...but she couldn't help the feelings hanging over her head. There was a feeling of dread, like she'd experienced this before and it had been bad.

Had that been the reason she'd forgotten? Shying away from the idea, she picked up a can of pineapple and put it on the shelf.

They finished putting away the groceries in a tense silence. Then he turned to her. "I need to go feed my stock."

She nodded at him and breathed a sigh of relief. As she watched him walk out to the stock pen, the quietness of the house surrounded her. She could hear the ticking of the mantle clock, the hum of the refrigerator when it came on, the sound of her own breathing.

Why had she worried about Rafe's reaction to her comment? Was there something in her past, the past she couldn't remember, that had to do with—

Suddenly being alone wasn't the haven she'd thought it would be. Unknown ghosts filled the room. And April had to decide which to face—the terrors of the past or the discomfort of the present.

She voted for the present and headed for the back door.

Rafe walked to the corral and brought out one of the carrots that he kept for his sorrel, Sam. The horse bit the carrot and chewed it happily.

"Well, Sam, it appears that something is bothering our mystery lady. She's acting like a skittish mare."

Rafe had noticed April's apprehension again at the sheriff's office. That had happened the night before, too. And there was her curious reaction to shopping. She acted like a scared kid. Once she'd understood it didn't bother him to spend his money, she let loose. It had warmed his heart to see her smile.

But again, when he mentioned the groceries, she got uptight. Over groceries, of all things. Now why would that bother her? Had it been his comment about his office that got the reaction?

Sam lowered his head, pushing up against Rafe's hand and bringing his master back to the present.

"So you're hungry, are you, big feller? Okay, I'll get your dinner ready."

Hurrying out the back door, April saw Rafe working at the entrance to the barn. "Would you mind if I came with you, after all?" she called out.

He paused in his chore. "Not at all." He picked up the bucket and headed into the barn. "We'll see if you know anything about ranching, won't we?"

"You're going to want me to do something?" Glancing around, she added, "Couldn't I just watch—which is what I had in mind? I might mess things up for you."

"You can do whatever you want."

His light comment made her smile and eased her mind, making her feel foolish for her earlier worries. "I think I'll just watch to begin with," she answered. Looking around, it was obvious to her that the barn was new.

Inside the main door, Rafe reached for the switch and flooded the inside with golden light, chasing away the twilight gloom. The sound of meows echoed through the building. April looked around for the source.

"Momma cat is in the far stall." Rafe nodded in that direction. "She just had a litter of kittens."

April walked to the end of the barn and saw a calico cat with six kittens nursing. The sight brought a smile to her face.

Rafe rested his arms on the upper edge of the stall. Oddly enough, his tall presence next to April now brought peace. Whatever had been bothering her before seemed to have disappeared. That flash of fear had been irrational. Not only did she have no memory, she seemed to be swinging like a pendulum, between fear and contentment.

He nodded at the cats. "It appears Patches's babies are greedy little things."

"And Momma doesn't seem to mind."

"Naw, not Patches. She's probably the most laid-back cat I've ever owned."

He filled the feeding trough with two flats of hay and a scoop of oats, then walked out to the corral. He guided his big sorrel into his stall. The horse poked his head back out and nudged April's arm. The horse's action unnerved her.

"He wants to be petted," Rafe informed her.

April eyed the animal, then looked at Rafe. Rafe took her hand in his, then guided it to the area between the horse's ears. "Scratch him there."

While April scratched the horse, Rafe went out and brought in the other horse.

"I guess it's kind of obvious that I'm not used to this," she commented as Rafe put up the other horse.

"Naw."

April gaped at him, then understood that he was teasing her. "Well, at least we know one more thing about me."

"I guess we do. You know about the history of the Rangers, but can't recall the modern history. You don't know jack about ranching, but you make a mean chili. And you sound like a Texan."

"It's not much."

He paused. "It's a good beginning, April."

As Rafe began to feed the goats and chickens, he handed her a basket. "Why don't you check and see if there are any eggs." He pointed to the nests.

She stared at each nest as if it housed a poisonous snake. "You sure? I mean, maybe the chickens won't like it."

A laugh escaped from his throat as he grabbed the basket used for collection. "Yep, it's obvious that you don't know anything about farming or ranching. You're probably a city girl."

She frowned at him. "I bet I'd probably know how to—" She couldn't think of anything she might know about the city.

"Yes?"

She frowned at him. What would a city girl know? "—drive in traffic."

"That'll put the fear of—" He didn't finish his thought.

Shrugging, she started gathering eggs. At the last nest, the chicken whose domain it was decided she didn't want her nest disturbed, and pecked at April's hand.

"Ouch," April yelled, yanking her hand back. "I thought you said the chickens wouldn't mind if I gathered the eggs?"

A guilty flush stained his cheeks. "I forgot about Stretch. She's one contrary bird. I've threatened her more than once with a stew pot. She still pecks me." He walked to April, took her hand and looked at the broken skin. "We'll need to clean that up and put some antiseptic on it."

"You sound like your sister."

"Well, any rancher out in this part of the state will tell you that you need to attend to things like that. Infection will set in and then you're in trouble."

"Gee, I didn't think I could get in anymore trouble," she grumbled.

"April, there's no limit to the trouble that could set in on you. Let's avoid this one." As Rafe walked back to the house, he stopped and eyed Stretch. "Do that again, bird, and you're a goner."

The chicken blinked and then strutted away.

Oddly, a warm feeling of being protected enveloped April as they reentered the kitchen. Rafe set the basket on the counter, grasped her hand and led her to the bathroom.

"It seems to me we've done this before," she said.

Rafe paused as he pulled items from the medicine chest above the sink. "You're right."

With his big body next to hers, the room seemed to shrink in size. She was aware of every inch of his six-foot-plus frame. And his hard muscles, which she vividly remembered from her ride on his horse. Although she couldn't remember her own name, she could describe in minute detail the breadth and strength of Rafe's legs and chest.

Oh rats, she was in trouble.

He washed the affected area, and handed her a towel. Then he squeezed out a small amount of antibacterial cream and gently rubbed it into her hand. She didn't notice any discomfort. She only felt the heat of his body next to hers, the touch of his palm on her. And all sorts of images came to mind.

She must have made a sound, because he looked up. "Did I hurt you?" There was such concern in his voice that all she wanted to do was lean close and cover his lips with her own.

What she was feeling must have shown on her face. Rafe slowly released her hand and stepped away. "I think that should cover it."

He didn't know the half of it. "Thank you," she managed to say, forcing the words through her embarrassment. It was odd to have a man care for her. She didn't have any memory, but there was a feeling deep in her soul that this man's concern was something she'd never come across.

She felt as if she were on a roller-coaster, up one minute, then plunging to earth the next. The question was, how did she remember there was such a thing as a roller-coaster when she couldn't recall her name?

"Are you hungry?"

Rafe's question was a welcome diversion from her thoughts. "Yes."

"Then why don't we go make dinner?"

"That's a good idea."

"After dinner, I'll check with the folks down in Austin—see if they've come up with a match for your prints."

April didn't know anymore whether she wanted to be found on that list or not.

They watched the local news as they fixed dinner. Being with April, working with her in the kitchen, brought a host of unbidden thoughts to Rafe's mind. How much he liked the feeling of sharing dinner chores with her. How much she filled up the vacant corners of his soul. How alone he'd been over the last few years. And how right it felt to have her here.

Each time he told himself he was asking for trouble, April would smile, or laugh at a local story on the news about a man getting caught crawling out of his neighbor's bedroom window when the husband came home early. Her laughter was like spring rain, cool and refreshing, bringing life to his cold heart.

After the meal was finished and the dishes were done, he turned to her. "Do you want to come with me and look at the missing persons lists?"

"You don't mind if I come in?"

"Why would I mind?"

"Well, you mentioned you like your office neat." Color stained her cheeks.

"Are you planning on trashing the place?"

Her eyes widened. "Of course not." There was a slight note of indignation in her voice, which made him smile.

"Then I don't have a problem with it."

"Oh."

They walked down the hall to his office. April paused at the entrance to his private world. He walked in and pulled a chair beside the desk.

"Sit down, and I'll turn on the computer and see if Austin has any answers for us."

April sat and folded her hands in her lap. He could see her knuckles go white with tension. He wanted to lay his hand over hers and comfort her, but he didn't dare. The heat between them was increasing, and common sense was telling him to keep his distance.

"Don't worry. No matter what we find, at least we'll know more than we do now."

She didn't look at him, but simply nodded her head.

It was the trembling of her lower lip that knocked a hole in his stomach.

Before he could turn on his machine, the phone rang. It was the DPS helicopter pilot, reporting that they hadn't located the missing car in their search that afternoon.

"Thanks, Mike," Rafe said, hanging up the phone. He told April about the results of the search, then added, "Hopefully, we can find something out another way."

Rafe turned on his machine, tapped in to the state computer, identified himself, and typed in the request for the results of the fingerprint match. Since he'd been okayed for access, he requested the results of the inquiry sent by the Brewster County sheriff on a "Jane Doe."

The screen blinked back that the match on Jane Doe had come back negative.

It was as if a weight had been lifted off his shoulders. April's eyes darted toward the screen. *Negative.* "Does that mean I'm not a criminal?"

"That's right, but it also means that you didn't work for the state."

"But what if I committed a crime in Louisiana? Or Kentucky, or—"

He laid his hand on hers. "We'll forward the prints to the FBI. That should help." He picked up the phone and, since it was so late, dialed Derek's home phone number.

Derek answered, and Rafe let him know what he'd discovered. "I forwarded the prints to the FBI to run through their computer."

"How'd your trip into Alpine go?" Derek asked.

"It didn't turn up anything. But April will be in the paper tomorrow, so be aware that you might get some calls on her."

"No problem."

Rafe hung up the phone. When he turned to April, he was surprised to find there were tears in her eyes. She swallowed, then stood and walked to the window. The darkness outside turned the window into a mirror, and he could see clearly the tears glistening on her cheeks.

Rafe knew he needed to stay away from April, but no matter how hard he tried, he couldn't ignore her pain. Standing, he walked up behind her, slipped his arms around her waist, and pulled her back against him.

Chapter 6

Rafe turned April around and tucked her close, his hands stroking her back, trying to comfort her. She fit exactly right into his arms.

The feel of her was rich, touching every one of his senses. Her face rested against his neck, and her cheek was smooth and heavenly, teasing him, making him want to touch more. Her lips brushed against his skin, mingling with her tears, creating an exquisite texture of sensations, making it hard to concentrate on anything else but the here and now.

It was as if her heart were breaking. Although Rafe knew it was a mistake, he couldn't stop himself—his hands softly brushed away the strands of hair stuck to her face.

"April, it's all right." They were lame words. Words he wasn't even sure were true.

Her eyes, filled with confusion, met his. As naturally as the sun setting in the west, he leaned down and with his hands framing her face, covered her mouth with his. It was as if she were dying from lack of water, and he were the cool drink that saved her. Her mouth flowered under his, inviting him to deepen the kiss. His tongue traced the seam of her lips, and immediately she opened her mouth, welcoming him in.

Her hands clutched his shirt, then slid up and around his neck.

He needed more contact. Walking her back a step, he pressed her into the side of the bookcase that stood by the window. Every inch of their bodies, from shoulders to knees, was pressed together.

When he reached for the buttons on her blouse, she made a sound—of pleasure or protest, he couldn't be sure—but he lifted his head long enough for sanity to return. Her gaze met his. He saw wanting in those green depths, but he also saw confusion—even fear. And that dashed his ardor more quickly than a bucket of cold water.

Stepping away, he gave her an uncomfortable smile. "Try not to worry, April. That won't help anything."

She nodded, but didn't meet his gaze.

"Why don't you take the first round in the bathroom, while I check on the stock outside." He didn't wait for her answer, but walked out into the night, praying that the drop in temperature would cool the heat in his blood.

April hurried into the bedroom, gathered up her tooth-brush and the T-shirt she'd slept in last night, and hob-bled back to the bathroom. She was going to take a bath and wash her hair. She felt grubby and irritable; maybe a bath would improve her frame of mind.

But afterward, April discovered that her attitude hadn't changed much. She was still tied up in knots, trying to forget what had happened between her and Rafe. Oh, it had started innocently enough: he had been trying to comfort her. But it had quickly escalated into something else entirely.

And she guessed that was what disturbed her the most. She was attracted to Rafe. When he looked at her, a thrill raced through her body. Every time she glanced at him, she remembered every kiss he'd given her. And she had much more now to recall and relive.

"Enough," she scolded herself. "This isn't helping anything, mooning over something you can't have. Stop it." She shook her head. If anyone overheard her, they would think she was losing her mind.

And that wasn't far from the truth.

Rafe looked at the night sky. The stars were wonderful out here in this sparsely populated part of Texas. There were no large cities around to hide them. The Milky Way was brilliant, reminding him of nights when he was a kid and sprawled out in the grass telling stories to his best friend.

Taking a deep breath, he considered the problem he had just escaped. He knew he had wanted to make love to April. But she was under his care, and she didn't need him panting after her like a stud bull. The problem was, the woman drew him like no other female ever had.

Well, he needed to reassure her that what just passed between them wouldn't happen again. She needed to know that. Ah, hell, who was he kidding? He needed to hear himself promise not to touch her.

One of the Angora goats that he kept poked her head out of the night pen, wanting him to pet her.

"You're a spoiled lady, Callie," he told the goat. "What am I going to do, huh?"

The goat calmly chewed, enjoying his attention.

"You're right, Callie. I messed up." He gave the goat a final pat, then turned and strode into the house. He walked through the kitchen, heading toward April's room. As he stepped into the hall, the bathroom door opened and there stood April, dressed only in his T-shirt. His body surged out of control. Again.

April's face turned red with embarrassment. "Uh—I forgot to get a nightgown and robe today, so I just…uh…used your T-shirt again. I hope you don't mind."

His eyes went over her body. Oh, no, he didn't mind. "Of course not. I wanted to tell you that what happened in my office a few minutes ago won't happen again. Things kind of got out of hand."

There was an odd look on her face, but it vanished quickly. "I understand."

"We don't know anything about you. I mean, if you're married or not."

She looked down at her empty left hand. There was no indication that she had recently worn a ring.

"I know there's no sign of a ring, but Alex doesn't often wear her wedding ring while she's practicing medicine. It's easier to leave her wedding ring at home. I know other married ladies who don't wear a ring. You could be one of them."

She shrugged, and it was obvious to Rafe that April didn't have anything on under that shirt. Things were going from bad to worse.

"Well, I want you to know you're safe with me." While he spoke, his eyes were fastened on her long, shapely legs.

Hypocrite, a voice in his head nagged. He expected

her to react with gratitude, but oddly enough she seemed disappointed.

"Thank you." She scurried around him and went into her room.

As the bedroom door closed, Rafe rested his head against the wall. He wondered if Alex's baby was still contagious, because he didn't think he should remain alone with April much longer—or he was going to have a lot more conversations with Callie.

Rafe looked down the hall toward his room and knew he wouldn't be able to sleep. Instead, he walked to his office and sat down at his desk. He logged onto his computer and checked the missing persons list again. After close to an hour of going over every list he could think of, Rafe leaned back in his chair. There'd been two women who were close to April's description, but when he called up picture IDs, it was obvious they didn't match.

Something wasn't right here. If he'd been married to April or if she'd been his sister, and she had been missing close to forty-eight hours, he would've been raising hell, putting her name on every list he could think of, rousing the police. So why hadn't someone reported her missing?

His gut clutched. There was something wrong here. It was screaming at him. But what?

He stood and walked to the window. This wasn't the first time he had had a strong feeling about a situation, but it was the first time his heart was involved.

And he didn't like it.

April dressed in the jeans and T-shirt that Rafe had purchased for her. She looked into the dresser mirror at the face that was still unfamiliar. It unnerved her every time she saw her own face. Why couldn't she remember who she was? And why....

She bowed her head and took a deep breath. She could spend all morning in here asking "what if" and "why," but what good would that do? Besides, she smelled the coffee brewing and wanted some.

Stepping into the hall, the image of Rafe kissing her filled her brain. She ached as she relived that scene and the accompanying feelings that had been with her all night.

As she entered the kitchen, she made herself sound cheerful and tried to put away the erotic memories. "Good morning," she greeted Rafe.

Rafe stood against the counter, drinking his coffee. He looked well rested and so appealing that she wanted to walk into his arms and let him surround her with his strength. When she could tear her eyes away from him, she noticed that he had placed another mug on the counter by the coffeemaker.

"Help yourself." He nodded toward the delicious brew.

After she poured herself a cup, he said, "I was thinking of driving into Saddle this morning. We could have breakfast at Mabel's and then pick up a newspaper and read the story they did on you. How's that sound?"

April was struck by the fact that this lawman was asking her opinion. For some reason, she felt it was a new experience for her. "That sounds fine to me."

Nodding to her ankle, he said, "How do you feel this morning?"

She glanced down. "It's still tender."

"I'll take you by the clinic and let Alex look at it."

"You don't have to do that. I'm sure she's busy."

Rafe grinned. "Yup, I'm sure you're not from around here."

She frowned. "What do you mean?"

"During the TB epidemic a couple of years ago, the clinic was busy. That was the last time Alex was busy morning 'til night. She'll be glad to see you."

"But it's Saturday."

Rafe shook his head. "Quit making excuses, April. Alex won't mind. Trust me."

She did.

Rafe stopped his truck in front of the newly remodeled post office. "I'll be back in a second with the newspaper."

He raced into the building. "Hey, Norma." He opened his post office box and got his mail and the newspaper.

"Rafe, that was some story in the paper this morning about your mystery guest. I guess it hasn't been long enough to get any reaction, has it?"

"That's right. But I'm hoping something will shake loose in the next couple of days."

Norma looked around. "So did you leave your mystery lady at home?"

"I call her April. She's out in the car if you want to meet her."

An expression of delight lit Norma's face. "I sure do. Why, we haven't had this much excitement since the doctor came to town."

Norma followed Rafe out to his truck.

"April, I want you to meet our postmistress, Norma Mayer."

Smiling, April reached through the open window and shook Norma's hand. "It's nice to meet you, Norma."

"Oh, my, how are you? Is it true that you don't re-member who you are? Why, that newspaper article sounded like you were on death's door. You look pretty good to me, except for that bruise on your head."

Rafe had to grin at Norma's eager questioning of April. But he was also interested in seeing April's re-action to it. April politely answered all Norma's ques-tions as best she could. Finally, after about five minutes, Rafe broke in. "Norma, we're going to Mabel's for breakfast. Would you like to join us?"

"Oh, my, I've been rattling on, haven't I? No, you two go to breakfast. I've already eaten." She walked back into the building.

Rafe climbed into the cab and handed April the news-paper. "Let's go eat and over breakfast we can read the article."

Rafe's truck and Alex's car pulled up to the clinic at the same time. "How do you feel this morning?" Alex asked April as she unlocked the door of the clinic.

"My ankle is sore this morning, more so than yester-day," she commented as she used the crutches to walk inside.

"Anything else?" she asked as she threw her purse on the desk. "Any headaches or some return of your memory?"

"I've got a headache, and occasionally I'll get a mem-ory or see a scene, but it's only for a moment."

"She remembers how to cook," Rafe offered.

"I'm sure that you appreciate that," Alex remarked. "But is there any headway on the return of your mem-ory?"

"No."

"Well, it's early yet. Don't give up hope. That article

in the newspaper this morning should help. If someone out there knows her, you will hear."

"That's what we hope," Rafe replied.

After a quick examination, Alex confirmed what they already knew: she was getting better. "I wish I could do more, but Mother Nature can't be beat. What April needs now is time to heal. She should put heat on that ankle today. I don't think she'll be dancing tonight at Dick's party, but the outing will be good for her."

"How's the baby?" Rafe asked. Sometimes, it was hard for him to believe he had this warm, loving family.

"Cranky. Derek's with her now. He'll be ready for me to take over, but I think I'll work a little here at the clinic before going home."

"Are you sure Derek's had chicken pox?"

"Yes. And what about you, Rafe? Did you have it?"

"You better know I did. It was a miserable two weeks for me."

Alex laughed. "If you need anything else, call."

"You got it."

April looked at herself in the mirror. The gauze dress flowed around her legs, soft and sensuous, making her feel pretty. Not wanting to call attention to the bruise at her temple, she had left her hair loose, falling around her shoulders.

She wasn't wearing makeup, but she had purchased a tube of lipstick at the grocery store and had applied the soft rose color to her lips.

The dress needed something to set it off, but she didn't have any jewelry.

What would Rafe think? He'd spent the day alternating between his office and the barn. She had the distinct feeling that he'd been trying to avoid her, a gesture she should have welcomed after the scorching kiss they had shared last night. But her heart wasn't buying any of her logical reasons. She wanted to talk to him, touch him, kiss him. He was the only solid thing in her bleak world.

Her face flamed at the thought of being wrapped in his arms, enjoying the feel of his lips, his body pressed intimately against hers. For some unknown reason, Rafe's strength didn't frighten her. She didn't question that she was safe with him. It was a belief she didn't want to examine too closely—why she felt that way with Rafe, but nervous with other lawmen.

"Get a grip," she murmured to her reflection in the mirror. "These feelings you're having aren't meant to be. You need to concentrate on recovering your memory."

With that last admonition, she nodded to herself, then opened the bedroom door.

Rafe was waiting for her in the living room. His back was turned to her as he looked out at the scenery, giving her a moment to observe him. He was dressed in a white cowboy shirt, tan slacks, and boots. His dark hair was a stark contrast to the shirt. He was so handsome that he took her breath away.

He turned and his gaze traveled over her, much as hers had him. When his eyes met hers, she read approval there. And interest.

"You're lovely in that." He nodded to the dress.

Her hands went to her neck. "It's kind of plain, but—thank you. For the dress and the compliment."

He held up his hand. "Wait a minute. I've got something to dress up that outfit." He disappeared down the hall. Several minutes later, he returned with a small purple pouch. He opened the draw string and shook out a silver-and-turquoise, squash-blossom necklace. It was a beautiful piece of work.

"Oh, Rafe, that is incredible," she breathed, running her fingers over the individual pieces.

"This was my mom's pride and joy. Turn around," he commanded her.

She looked at him. "Surely not. You need to save that for your future wife."

"I wouldn't have let my ex-wife near this."

"But—"

"Turn around, April. Wear it tonight for me."

Her eyes held his for a moment, then she turned around and swept her hair out of the way.

The necklace was heavy when he placed it around her neck. His fingers quickly closed the clasp, then lingered for a moment at the base of her neck, setting off fireworks up and down her spine. When he stepped away, she turned.

"How does it look?" She glanced down at the unique piece.

"My mom would be delighted that you're wearing it."

Her fingers ran over the cool metal. The weight of the necklace was reassuring.

"There's something else here, too," he said, digging down into the pouch again and pulling out matching earrings. They were for pierced ears. He looked at her ear lobes. "I think you can wear these."

He handed them to her. April hurried into the bathroom, cleaned the earrings and put them on. The woman who stared back at her from the mirror had eyes that shone with excitement and smiled in delight at the picture she made.

Guard your heart, the thought flashed through her

brain. *You don't know anything more today than you did last night. Be careful.*

April's fingers touched the necklace, and she knew then that she was losing the battle to stay uninvolved.

Rafe turned on his truck's radio to a station in Marfa that played country and western.

April hadn't said too much after she'd come out of the bathroom, but she had glowed with pleasure. The necklace had been left to him by his mother with instructions to give it to his future wife. When he'd seen April standing there, looking like an angel, he'd known that the necklace was perfect for her tonight. Too bad he had all sorts of other feelings about April that he shouldn't be having. Damn, why couldn't he keep his feelings where they belonged—out of this situation?

"Most everyone from around this area, for at least fifty miles, will be at Dick's barbecue. We're celebrating the end of winter and the beginning of spring. It's a time we can see each other after the winter, and before the rough work for spring begins. You should be big news at the barbecue, since the article appeared in the newspaper this morning," he added, glancing at her.

"I was hoping that we might have gotten a call today." From her tone, it was obvious that April was disappointed with the lack of reaction thus far.

"Don't worry about that. People don't get their newspapers until they come into town to pick up their mail. It might take a couple of weeks for everyone in the county to see that article. Sometimes word of mouth is the most effective tool. That probably hasn't changed in a hundred years. Of course, how that information gets out—telephones, computers, faxes—that has changed."

He noticed April's fingers sliding over the necklace.

"I'm trying to be calm about this," she said, "but I'm nervous. It's like riding a roller-coaster. The wait nearly kills you."

He glanced at her. "You remembering, April?"

Her eyes widened in surprise. "You're right. How would I know what it feels like to be on a roller-coaster, if I hadn't been on one before?"

"Can you remember anything about the roller-coaster you were on?"

She closed her eyes, and he could see her trying to conjure a picture of the place where the coaster was. It was frustrating not to be able to do something for April. All he could do was wait.

"It overlooked a lake of some kind. And it must've been an amusement park."

"Good. Can you see any signs around the coaster? Or maybe some sign in the distance when you were on the ride?"

She was quiet for a long time, then said, "No." Her voice sounded discouraged.

"Each bit of information that occurs to you, April, is another piece of the puzzle to your past. Don't be discouraged. More and more of the picture is coming together. Maybe in the next few days, there will be enough to lead us to your identity."

"How can you be so positive?" Her question was a plea for reassurance.

"I've worked with less and still made identifications." He'd also had more, but come up short. But he wouldn't mention that to her. There was no need to worry her any more.

He pulled off the county road and turned onto the gravel drive that led to Dick's large ranch house. He noticed her hands folded in her lap, her knuckles were pale.

"I met Dick nearly 12 years ago when I first moved out here. He was my uncle's friend. Helped me learn the cattle business. Growing up in the valley, I didn't know too much about cattle. I knew about picking grapefruit and oranges and other seasonal fruit and vegetables, but herding cows is mighty different from what I was used to."

That brought a smile to her lips. "Picking grapefruit?"

"Sure. When the grower needs to get the grapefruit off the trees, he's hiring. Doesn't matter if you're a skinny kid, all arms and legs. Hey, but it pays. Of course, my mom made me go to school, then I could join the picking crew after school. Fortunately for me, the crew foreman let me come late and just paid me for what I picked. That's when I discovered that education was the way out. My mom had been telling me that, but—" He glanced at her and smiled. "Well, let's just say I was hardheaded. The best way to teach me was the school of hard knocks."

"So you're telling me you are stubborn?"

"My mom used to call me a—" a frown crossed his brow "—donkey is probably the closest translation."

Her laughter rang through the cab, doing all sorts of things to his blood pressure. He wanted to hear her laugh more.

"So how did you end up out here?"

"I told you, remember?"

"Oh, yes, your uncle left you the ranch."

"It was no problem to get reassigned out here. Unfortunately, when I took over the ranch, I didn't know a thing about ranching. My uncle had this contrary bull.

He didn't much care for me. And he didn't want me messing around in his love life.''

"So what did you do?"

"Are you really interested or just being polite?'' he asked her.

"I was just wondering how you overcame the problem. Obviously, you couldn't draw your gun and tell that bull you were a Ranger and to behave.''

He laughed. "I never thought of that. But with that bull, it wouldn't have mattered.''

"So how did you deal with the situation?"

"Well, Dick told me how to redirect that stubborn critter, so that bull was fixated on the female and didn't give a snort about me. Hormones are powerful things.'' He grinned.

And right now, he thought, he could truly sympathize with that bull.

Chapter 7

There at the base of the mountain stood the ranch. Cars were parked haphazardly in front of the main house. Rafe found a parking space and helped April out. They had decided that since her ankle was feeling better, she would leave the crutches behind. As he led her toward the main door, they heard voices in the backyard. Feeling April's hesitation, Rafe smiled at her and pulled her hand onto his arm.

"Are you okay?" he asked her.

She nodded.

He didn't bother with the front door, but walked April around the house to the patio.

"Hey, Rafe, good to see you," Dick called out. He hurried to the new arrivals' side. "And you brought the mystery lady."

April smiled at the older man. "Hello. It's nice to see you again."

"It was an interesting article in the paper this morning. Have you heard anything as a result?" Dick asked.

"Not so far. But, as I was explaining to April, it sometimes takes a while for folks to read their papers, with their work and all. Sunday's usually read-the-paper day for most ranchers."

"Well, I can take care of the neighbors who are here." Dick turned and cleared his throat. "I want y'all to meet a local celebrity that we have in our midst. If you don't know, Rafe found our mystery lady on the farm road near his ranch. She was without a car and had been caught in one of the flash floods we had a couple of days ago. She doesn't know who she is. Rafe wants to know if anyone was expecting company, or maybe she's a relative visiting family. So, if you know anything about her, come up and speak to Rafe."

"Also," Rafe added, "we're looking for April's car. If you see it, call either me or Derek."

"What kind of car?" Sal Melvin asked.

Rafe raised his eyebrow and stared at Sal. "Now, Sal, if the lady can't remember who she is or where she came from or how she appeared on my land, what makes you think she'd remember the kind of car she drove?"

Laughter rumbled through the crowd. Sal smiled sheepishly. "Hadn't thought about that."

"Does anyone else have a question?" Rafe look around.

"When did you find her?" a woman asked.

"I found April on Thursday morning."

The woman nodded.

"I thought you didn't know who she was," a man in the crowd yelled.

"We don't. My wife named her April," Derek explained.

There were murmurs throughout the room.

Rafe made it a point throughout the evening to introduce April to everyone at the party. No one was expecting a visitor. Nor did anyone know of anyone coming for a visit. Oddly enough, April seemed at ease with everyone but Derek. And when Wes Clayton arrived at the party, April stiffened visibly.

It was obvious that April disliked sheriffs. The question that nagged him was why? If she'd had personal trouble with a sheriff or saw a sheriff doing something wrong, the best person to go to in the state was a Ranger. And that gave the situation an entirely different spin: police corruption.

"Well, that was a waste of time," April sighed as they drove away from the party. "We don't know anything more now than we did before."

"Sure we do. I told you before, April, that a lot of good police work is eliminating possibilities."

"I know, but—"

"You were wanting a magic bullet, huh, and to know everything about yourself."

"It can't hurt to hope."

"I wonder if you've always been impatient."

"Wouldn't *you* be if you were in my shoes?"

He thought about it for a minute. "It's hard to know. Maybe we can come up with another way of identifying you."

That caught her interest. "How?"

"Well, remember me telling you that sometimes I work with bodies?"

She grimaced. "Yes."

He immediately regretted the manner in which he'd started his explanation, but had to continue. "We look for identifying marks on the body. So, do you have any scars?''

April thought about it. When she'd showered last night, she'd noticed a small scar on her abdomen. ''There's a small one on my stomach.''

He looked at the area she mentioned. ''Where?''

She pointed to the area to the right of her navel. ''It's right here.''

''What does it look like?''

''It's a couple of inches long. It's not very big. I wondered about it last night.''

''Well, I know just the person to call and ask about it.''

She frowned, then turned to him. ''Your sister?''

''She'll know. Is it an old scar?'' he asked.

''I think so. It wasn't pink. The skin around it was tan.''

Her words conjured up mental images that he didn't want to have. ''Were there any other marks or scars?''

She frowned. ''Well, I couldn't see everything. There might be something on my back, but someone would need to check for me.''

Oh, he didn't think so. So far, he hadn't been able to disassociate himself enough from the case to look at things logically and without emotion. If he looked at April's back, he knew he wouldn't be able to keep his objectivity. No, maybe he ought to call Alex and ask her if she had noticed any other marks on April. And then Alex could also identify the scar on April's stomach.

The instant they were in the house, Rafe walked to his office. Turning on the light on his desk, he picked up the phone and dialed Alex's home phone. April trailed behind him, lingering at the doorway. He noticed her unease but motioned her further into the room.

"Hi, sis," he said when Alex picked up. "I missed seeing you at the party."

"The baby's not contagious anymore, but I didn't want to leave her. The mother in me won out over the logical side of my brain."

"I understand. I need to ask you something. When you examined April the other day, did you notice any scars or distinguishing marks on her body?"

"Umm, let me think. There was a scar on her stomach. But other than that—oh, Rafe, that's a great idea. Why didn't I think of it? That scar tells us a lot."

"How's that?"

"That little scar probably came from some kind of laproscopic surgery. It's a specialized surgery that's only done at the larger hospitals in the state. You could fax a copy of a picture of April and a description of the scar to the bigger hospitals and have them put it up in the doctor's lounge, and see if any of the surgeons recognize her."

"Thanks for the information, Alex. I'll do that tomorrow morning." When he hung up the phone, he looked at April, who was hovering nearby.

"What did she say?"

Rafe explained. "I'll take a picture of you with my camcorder, then use the program I have to convert it to a picture in my computer. Faxing it to the hospitals won't be a problem."

April's eyes were wide. "I'm impressed with your technological knowledge."

"It's still a lot of legwork. Checking out leads, calling a dozen different numbers to trace information."

They spent the next hour putting together the pictures and text that Rafe wanted to fax to the hospitals. When the package was ready to go, Rafe dialed the Ranger

headquarters in Austin and faxed them the information.
The Rangers would put out an alert on her. If anyone
ran across information on a woman fitting April's description, they would know where to find her.

April watched in rapt attention as Rafe faxed the hospitals in San Antonio and El Paso.

When the last fax was sent, Rafe leaned back in his
chair. "Now, we wait."

A yawn caught April by surprise. "Oh, my, I'm more
tired that I realized."

He grinned. "The last couple of days have been
eventful for you. It's to be expected."

"You're right. Good night, Rafe." Her soft voice caressed him, making him want things that couldn't be.
She reached up and took off the squash-blossom necklace, then the earrings, and handed them to him. Her
fingers brushed his hand. "Thank you for the privilege
of wearing these. I know your mother must've been
proud to wear such a beautiful set."

His gaze held hers. "Good night, April."

He listened as she walked down the hall, then, when
he heard the door to her room close, went back to his
computer. Again he carefully checked missing persons
lists, state and national. There still was no one matching
April's description, and the longer it went without someone reporting April as missing, the more ominous the
situation became.

Something was going on here. He knew it, could feel
it. But what?

There were several pieces of the puzzle of April's
identity that were still missing. But he felt confident that
those pieces would soon fall into place.

April didn't sleep well. She woke several times, her
heart racing with fear. Dawn was a welcome glow on

the horizon. She dressed and was out of her room before the sun broke out. Rafe was already in the kitchen, fixing the coffee.

"Morning," he greeted her. "How did you sleep?"

She didn't want to go into why she hadn't rested. Shrugging, she murmured, "Okay."

Rafe leaned close and his gaze captured hers. "When you knew who you were, I bet you weren't a good liar."

Her eyes widened in surprise. "Why would you say that?"

"Because you're a lousy one now."

She opened her mouth, then closed it.

"See what I mean? Even now you can't deny I caught you in a little lie. You didn't sleep worth beans."

A scowl darkened her face. "I don't know what you're talking about."

Rafe laughed. "I wish all the folks I deal with were as transparent as you. It would make my job a lot easier. But mostly, I'm used to first-rate liars and con men. Running into you restores my faith in human nature."

A smile appeared on her face, like the sun peeking through the clouds. "Do you want to scramble the eggs or do you want me to do it?"

"Maybe you should cook them. Your chili was much better than mine."

"I think I've been had." There was laughter in her voice, which made Rafe grin.

"While you're doing that, I'll fix everything else."

"Deal."

They worked quietly, side by side. Rafe found himself comparing this experience with that of his marriage. His wife hadn't wanted to be anywhere near the kitchen. She'd wanted someone to wait on her. But he had been busy trying to establish himself in the department, so couldn't take off and play housekeeper. Nor was he rich enough to hire someone to attend her.

The real trouble was that Rafe found he hadn't wanted to try with Carmen. The fire that had blazed between them hadn't lasted very long after they'd married.

In contrast, the easiness he shared with April was comforting. And deadly. He couldn't afford this closeness.

"Eggs are ready. Got the plates?" April asked, breaking into his rehash of the past.

He took the plates to her, and after she dished out the eggs, carried them to the table. With his first bite, he knew his decision to let her cook was the right one. "You're better than I am, April. Want the job of cook while you're here?"

She paused in scooping up her egg. "Yes, I think I'd like that. Makes me feel like I'm at least helping and not just taking."

"And that's important for you?"

April thought about his question, then nodded. "Yes, it is. I want to feel useful. I mean, I might not remember who I am, but I want to pull my weight. It doesn't make sense, but I don't want to be coddled."

"Then you've got the job."

Too bad the vision of other things entered his brain. "Would you like to see my ranch today?" he asked, hoping to concentrate on something besides April.

"Sure. I wouldn't mind a ride."

"Then let me load the truck, then we'll be off."

"I'll be out in a minute."

Rafe nodded, then went outside to load his pickup with feed and hook the horse trailer to the truck.

* * *

April met him out in the barn, dressed in jeans, a white shirt, tennis shoes and with her hair pulled back into a ponytail.

He was dressed similarly in jeans and a western shirt. But the boots and tan Stetson told the story: he was a rancher, one of those men who spoke sparingly, but had a heart as deep and wide as Texas.

Where had that come from? she wondered.

"My, my, you look like a real cowgirl in that outfit." He smiled as he studied her, making her heart pick up tempo.

"I was just thinking the same thing about you."

"I look like a cowgirl?"

She laughed. "No, a cowboy. You know, the kind you see in the movies." She glanced down at herself. Pointing to his boots, she said, "Maybe I need a pair of those."

"When your ankle is better, I'll drive you into Alpine and we'll buy you a pair of Ropers."

"No, you've spent too much already."

He didn't argue the point. Instead, he loaded his horse into the trailer behind his pickup. "What are you doing?" she asked.

"Getting ready to feed the cattle."

"Why do you need both a horse and truck?"

"Well, we'll drive out and feed the cows. I'll count the heads and if I'm missing some animals, then I'll use the horse to go looking for the strays."

"Seems like a lot of work."

Rafe nodded. "You're right." He untied the other horse and led it into the trailer.

"Why are you doing that?"

Emerging from the interior, he closed the trailer door. "I thought you might like to ride with me."

"Well, I'm not sure what kind of a rider I am."

"Don't worry about it. I saddled a gentle mare that won't give you any problems. Missy is a steady ride. Trust me."

She studied him for several moments, then nodded her head. "I do trust you."

Her words hung in the air between them, filled with more meaning than she had intended.

She shook her head and stood. "But remember, I don't know squat."

He laughed. "Somehow, April, I think you'll make it."

"We'll see."

He walked around the truck and opened the passenger door. "Hop in and we'll get going."

After she was seated, he rounded the truck and slid behind the wheel. He pointed to the battered Stetson on the seat between them. "That's for you. You'll need it to keep the sun off your head."

She picked up the hat and put it on. It was big and slid down to her eyebrows. A laugh escaped her lips. "Where did you get this?"

"One of the men who worked on the ranch part time left it behind when he quit. I thought it might fit you."

She glanced in the rearview mirror. "As a fashion statement, it lacks something."

"It's strictly protection."

Glancing in the rearview mirror again, April noticed the rifle on the rack behind her. "Is that for protection, too?"

"That, and if I come across a badly hurt cow...."

The color drained from her face.

Rafe started the engine and drove away from the barn. As April stared out the window of the truck, she was amazed at how sensitive Rafe had been to her reaction. She was grateful.

They drove for a good fifteen minutes. Finally, April looked at him in stunned amazement. "Where are these cows?"

He topped a small rise and came to a halt in the middle of the road. He then honked the horn several times. She threw him a curious look.

"Wait and see."

He got out of the truck, hopped into the bed and pushed several bales of feed onto the ground. He then walked back to the trailer and unloaded both horses. By the time he was done, twenty cows had come out of the brush and gullies around them. April got out of the truck and watched in surprise as the cows began to eat the feed Rafe had provided.

He counted the cows. "I'm missing a couple. I need to check the area around here to make sure they're not in trouble."

"How do you know?" she asked, looking at the cows feeding. "They look so much alike."

"I know each cow by name. I'm missing a couple who are out in this region. Besides, don't you want your riding lesson?"

She looked indignant. "How do you know I don't know how to ride?"

He tried to swallow his grin. Holding up his hands, he said, "Okay, we'll see if you know what you're doing."

Unloading the horses, he brought them around to the front of the trailer.

"This is Missy. You remember how I introduced you to Sam, my mount, last night."

"Yes."

"Do that for Missy." April shrugged, stepped close to the horse and rubbed her between her eyes.

After the introduction, Rafe helped April into the saddle. Rafe eyed how she was sitting. "This stirrup is too long. Let me shorten it for you."

He nudged her leg aside and shortened the strap. It was disconcerting to have his cheek next to her thigh. It was so intimate that other activities came to mind. She looked away, trying not to blush at her thoughts as Rafe rebuckled the stirrup, then placed her foot into it.

"There, that should be the right length," he said, his hand resting on her ankle. She nearly jumped out of her skin. It was amazing how sensitive an ankle could be. He walked around the horse and worked on the other stirrup. As his head was bent, April had the crazy urge to take off his hat and run her fingers through his hair.

What was wrong with her, lusting after Rafe this way? *Nothing* said the voice in her head. He was a man and she was a woman. Yeah, but a woman with no past, and a vague future. Rafe didn't need that.

"That's it." He looked up and caught her staring. Her face flooded with warmth.

He stepped into his saddle and threw his leg over the horse's back. His tight jeans outlined his backside in clear detail.

He showed her how to rein her mount and watched her carry out his instructions.

"Ready?"

"I hope so."

After several minutes, she grumbled, "I don't believe I've done this too often in the past."

"Don't you worry about it. Missy and I will take good care of you."

They were words that warmed her heart.

In the end, Rafe knew what he was talking about. Missy turned out to be an easy horse with an even temperament that made April feel at ease.

The earlier rains had made the land come alive with green. Small wildflowers were blooming, delicate and fragile.

"This is beautiful," she murmured, looking around the uneven land.

"This land after spring rains is a paradise. Long about September things are dry. It looks like one of those old pictures done in sepia."

April threw him a look of amazement. "Sepia?"

"You know, those old pictures that were done in tones of brown."

"I know what you were talking about. It's just that I didn't expect you to be so—"

"Knowledgeable?"

She felt the flush run up her neck. "I guess I was making an assumption. It's just that I didn't expect...I'm going from bad to worse."

"Don't worry about it. I have an interest in photography. I'm also interested in saving old photos—restoring them. A lot of the folks in the area come to me to save their photos."

"Really?"

"Do you find that odd?"

"Well, yeah. I mean you're a Ranger and a rancher and when you think of those occupations, you don't think photography."

"Then you don't know about the modern day Rangers. We have to take crime scene photos and do analysis on pictures and other aspects of the job."

She laughed. "You've nailed my problem, Rafe."

He reined in his horse and looked at her. "That's the

first time you've called me by my name." *It sounds good on your lips.* He didn't say the last words, but April swore she saw them in his eyes. It certainly was in the tone of his voice, dark and rich.

Embarrassed by her thoughts, she looked around at the scenery. "Someone should take a picture of this. Or better, capture it on canvas."

Rafe looked surprised. "Well, I'll leave that to someone else. I've got my hands full."

They rode back to the trailer in silence and loaded the horses, then drove back to the ranch—the windows down, the breeze refreshing and cool.

When they parked, Rafe walked around the front of the truck and opened April's door. Suddenly, a glint of light appeared on the horizon beyond the barn.

"April, get down!" Before she could react, he pushed her down onto the seat.

A shot echoed through the air. Rafe grunted and hopped into the seat next to her. Several other shots peppered the area around the truck. Rafe reached for the rifle on the rack behind them.

The roar of an engine sounded, then a vehicle drove off.

April looked at him with dazed eyes. "Why did that happen? I mean who would want to kill us?"

Rafe looked at her. "That's the $64,000 question. Why did someone want us dead?" He said "us," but she knew he meant "her."

A chill descended on her soul.

Chapter 8

Whoever was shooting at them was after April. Rafe had been too easy a target when he walked around the truck, and the shooter hadn't hit him. Only as he opened the door for April had the shooter sighted her.

Who'd been shooting at April? And why?

The newspaper article came to mind.

He listened carefully, trying to determine if he could hear the sounds of a car returning or anything out of the ordinary. Looking around again, he got out of the truck. His right leg buckled, and he would've fallen on his face if he hadn't been holding onto the door.

He heard the horses in the trailer; Missy was stomping. Sam, who was used to the sound of firearms, was quiet.

April slipped out of the truck. "Rafe are you all right?" Her eyes searched his face, then his body. She spotted the hole in his jeans. "You've been wounded."

He waved away her concern. "We need to get inside."

She wrapped her arm around his waist. "I'll help you." Her eyes were full of misery.

He took his rifle—he wasn't going to be caught unarmed again. As they walked toward the house, Rafe paused by the rear of his truck. "He shot out my damned tire." He looked back at his vehicle, noting several dents and holes in the sheet metal.

"Rafe, you're the one hurt." The agony in her voice was more painful to Rafe than his damn wound.

He closed his eyes. The wound throbbed like hell. He glanced down at his right thigh. At least there wasn't much blood, which meant the bullet hadn't caught a blood vessel.

They hurried to the back door, then went inside. She helped him into a chair by the table. Immediately, she went to the phone and called the sheriff's office. When Derek answered, April explained what had happened.

"Stay inside, April," Derek told her. "I'll bring Alex with me to see to Rafe."

When she hung up, she said, "Help's on the way."

April fell to her knees and tried to see the damage done.

The hole in his jeans was mute testimony of what had happened. April went white, and her eyes became glassy. She looked as if she were going to faint.

"April, are you all right?" Rafe asked, concerned more about her reaction than his own wound.

"I'm okay." She seemed to snap back. "What can I do?"

"You've done it—called for help."

"This is my fault, isn't it. Whoever was shooting was aiming at me, weren't they?"

"Don't worry, April. You can't change anything."

She stood and wrapped her arms around her waist.

It seemed like hours, but within fifteen minutes, they heard the sound of sirens, then doors slamming and a woman's voice calling, "Rafe, Rafe, where are you?"

"In here."

Alex raced into the house, followed by her husband, Derek.

Instantly, she knelt in front of Rafe. "This isn't exactly why I moved to Saddle, Rafe. I had enough of emergency medicine while I was in Houston and Bosnia."

He grinned. "Sorry, sis."

"What happened?" Derek asked.

Rafe explained how they were shot at.

"I'll check over the area," the deputy responded, immediately moving toward the door.

"Derek, when you finish, can you unload my horses from the trailer? The gunman got to us before I could get the horses out."

Derek disappeared out the back door.

Alex took out a pair of scissors out of her bag and Rafe held up his hand. "What are you doing? These are new jeans."

"I've got to see to the wound. Do you want to take the jeans off the other way?"

"Yeah. I can use these to work the cattle."

Alex rolled her eyes and looked at April. "I guess he'll live."

If he was worried about his jeans, then he couldn't be too badly hurt, could he? April wondered.

"Why don't we get you into your room? Then you can shuck your jeans and I can look at the wound," Alex said.

He nodded and let both women help him to the bedroom. He paused by the bed, when April's hands went to his waistband. His hands covered hers. He had dreamed of having April's hands there, but this wasn't exactly the scenario he had in mind.

"I think Derek might need help with the horses," he softly told her.

"But, I want—" April began.

"Sam and Missy might be nervous with those shots and Derek will need some help. Alex has control of everything here."

April hesitated for a moment, looking at Rafe. He attempted a smile.

"I'm in good hands, here. Alex is a trained E.R. doctor. Why don't you go help Derek?"

She looked as if she wanted to argue, but then nodded her head. "I'm sorry," she whispered, before she walked down the hall.

"What was that all about?" Alex asked once they were alone.

"Whoever was shooting at us was aiming for April."

Alex didn't look pleased. "I hope you know what you're doing."

"I do."

"Do you need help with those jeans?" Alex asked.

"I can undo my own jeans," Rafe grumbled as he reached for the snap. He pushed them over his hips, but stopped when the material brushed against his wound. He didn't say anything, but his eyes drifted closed.

"This is ridiculous, Rafe," Alex said. "Let me cut them off."

His eyes snapped open. "No."

"Well, all I have to say is you're more like Dad than you know," she grumbled.

Rafe didn't look pleased. Gingerly, he sat on the bed.

Alex looked at his boots and shook her head. "They have to come off."

Rafe nodded. Alex pulled off his boots and jeans. Rafe didn't make a sound, but his face was white and beads of sweat had gathered on his forehead. She raced into the bathroom, gathered up several towels and placed them under his thigh.

Alex carefully examined the wound. After several minutes she glanced up.

"Well, you're one lucky Ranger. The bullet only caught the fleshy part of your thigh. I'll clean it up and put some antibiotic cream on it. But you need to have a tetanus shot."

"But I just—"

"I looked at your records, Rafe. It's been long enough. You need another. And I brought one with me."

It took only a short time for Alex to clean and wrap Rafe's wound and give him the tetanus shot.

"Well, that should do it." She pulled out the antibiotic pills she'd brought with her. "You need to take these to make sure you don't get a secondary infection. The directions are on the container."

Rafe reached for his jeans.

Alex rested her hands on her hips. "What are you doing?"

"I'm getting dressed."

"No, you're not. You need to go to bed. Tomorrow will be soon enough for you to be up."

"I don't want to go to bed."

"Fine. Go sit on the couch in the living room, but you need to stay put for the night. Why don't I get you some sweatpants, and you can slip them on?"

He didn't look pleased.

"I'm sure April will appreciate it if you get dressed. Her eyes were as big as saucers when you started to unzip your jeans."

Finally, he nodded. "I've got some sweats on the top shelf in the closet."

"I'll get them for you."

"I'm not the only one who is like Dad, Alexandra," Rafe grumbled.

A laugh floated back to him.

April helped Derek unload the horses. As she walked Missy into the barn, Derek followed with Sam.

"What can you remember about what happened, April?"

Although she knew Derek was a friend, she couldn't help the shudder that raced through her. She couldn't say if her reaction was due to recalling the incident or to being this close to Derek. "I didn't see anything. As I was getting out of the truck, there was a loud sound. Rafe pushed me down on the seat. That's when he got shot. While we were hiding inside the cab, there were several other shots. I think one hit the tire on the truck." She couldn't help the despair filling her voice. "This has got to be my fault."

Derek put Sam in his stall and began to unsaddle him. "You don't know that, April."

"When was the last time someone shot at Rafe?" she demanded.

Glancing up from where he was unbuckling the saddle, he answered, "Two years ago. Rafe was shot several times by a felon he was tracking."

"Oh."

"Why don't you unsaddle Missy? Just follow what I've done with Sam."

"Okay." She was successful until she got to the bridle. "I think I've gone as far as I can."

Derek stepped to her side. "I'll take over from here."

April moved away and let Derek go about his job.

"Has anything come back to you? I mean, do you recall any part of your past?"

She didn't mention the flashback she had experienced earlier when she looked at Rafe's wound. She'd seen another man, lying in a pool of blood on the floor. Now she shied away from admitting what she had recalled, not ready to face the memory. "I keep thinking that I'll wake up from this dream and that everything will be all right. That I'll have a past, a family, a job. But I keep waking up and the nightmare is real."

When Derek was finished, he watered the horses. April was amazed that she had become so fond of Missy. She laid her cheek on Missy's warm neck.

"You look like a natural there, April," Derek said, walking to where she stood.

"You know, it feels right, standing here." She shook off the feeling and stepped away from Missy. "Of course, when Rafe took me riding earlier, it was obvious that I hadn't done it before."

"Let's go inside and see how Rafe's doing."

April nodded. She was eager to make sure Rafe was all right.

"All the bullets are pretty chewed up," Derek told Rafe, handing him the shells that he had dug out of the side of the house and fence post. Derek and Rafe had closed themselves in his study to talk about the afternoon's events. "I'll take your tire into town with me and have Billy recover that bullet, but I don't think it will tell us too much."

Rafe rubbed his arm over the ache in his thigh. "Yeah, whoever was shooting at us meant business."

"Could be. You want me to send this to the Ranger's lab?" Derek asked.

"Yup. I'm also going to call my commander and tell him what's happened. He needs to know about this development. He wasn't too happy about me keeping April here with me. But I told him that it was the easiest way all around. One more thing, has that stranger that Mabel talked about shown up in town again?"

"No one's seen hide nor hair of him. You know, this incident could've been sparked by that newspaper article that came out yesterday morning." Derek frowned. "Maybe someone doesn't want April to remember. She might have seen something she shouldn't have."

Running his hands through his hair, Rafe sighed. "I've thought about that."

"And you agree?"

"Yeah, I think you have a point." He didn't like it one bit that his idea of doing the newspaper interview had brought about this action against April. "I think she's in trouble."

"Are you going to say anything to April about it?" Derek asked.

"You bet. I don't want to put her in danger. After what happened today, we'll need to be careful for the next few days while we wait on a response to our hospital ads and the newspaper article. We've already shaken something loose. Let's just keep our fingers crossed that some good leads turn up."

Derek picked up the sheet of paper from the desk. "Have you checked the missing persons reports today?"

"I checked before April and I went out to feed the cattle. There still was nothing...which I can't understand. If Alex was missing, wouldn't you move heaven and earth to try to find her?''

"I would, but then again, I love my wife. If I wanted to kill her, I wouldn't report her missing.''

The words hung like a pall in the room.

"I thought the same thing. What happened thi   er-noon only gives that suspicion credence.''

Rafe pulled out a padded envelope and began   dress it to the Ranger lab.

Derek leaned against the desk. "Have you notic   at every time I get within a hundred yards of Ap   she tenses up?'' he asked. "Why, in the barn a few n   tes ago, when I got near her, I thought she was g   to jump out of her skin. Is it me or is she like th   ith everyone?''

"It's you,'' Rafe answered. Pausing, he glan   ed up and saw Derek staring at him. "It's not so much you as your position as a deputy. April was that tense with Wes at the main office in Alpine.''

"And she isn't that wary of you?''

Rafe couldn't help the grin that split his face. "I guess I'm a nice guy.''

Derek cursed.

A laugh erupted from Rafe's throat. "Does my sister know you talk like that?''

That earned him another glare.

Rafe held up his hands. "Okay, okay. No, what I noticed is that everyone with the sheriff's department seem to make April tense up. I've also noticed that when she was in my office last night and we made up those pictures to send to the hospitals, she was nervous about the neatness.''

"So, my guess is that a neat sheriff would send April into orbit,'' Derek teased.

Rafe shook his head. A neat sheriff. But as he thought about it, that might be the problem. "Derek, you might've hit the nail on the head."

"What, that we need to investigate the neat sheriffs in the state?"

"No, but I think that the sheriff's department and neatness has something to do with April's past. Just keep your eyes open and know what we're looking for."

"Do you know how many counties there are in the state?" Derek asked.

"A lot."

"Two-hundred-forty-five."

"Then we've narrowed the search down from a million possibilities to a couple of hundred. Sounds like a winner to me. Also, listening to April speak, I'd say she was a Texan, but comes from an urban area. That might help narrow our search to sheriffs in the middle of the state."

Derek nodded. "I think you're right. I've got a couple of friends who are sheriffs or working in sheriffs' offices. I'll contact them—see what they come up with."

"I'll also notify my commander what we suspect."

Rafe handed Derek the padded mailer.

"I'll give this to our postmistress when I get back." Tucking the envelope under his arm, Derek looked at Rafe. "You know, today is the first time I've ever heard you refer to Alexandra as your sister. She thinks the world of you."

Rafe looked down at his leg. "She's a fine doctor. And I'm proud she's my sister."

"I've noticed something else," Derek added with a grin. "You seem to have come down with the same symptoms I had last year."

"What's that?" Rafe knew only that it had been the

talk of the county for quite some time that Dr. Alexandra Courtland's car had broken down in Saddle. While her car had been fixed, Alex had looked at the mechanic's sick mother and discovered the TB that had raced through the town. Derek and Alex had fallen in love during that time.

"Well, during the TB epidemic, I found myself stuck in my house with Alex, the way you are with April. My eyes always tracked her and my body knew where she was every second of the time we were together. I'm afraid it didn't get better, only worse. But—" he winked "—the cure wasn't fatal. C'mon, let's go mingle with the ladies."

Derek offered Rafe his hand. He took it and tried not to put pressure on his bad leg. What Derek had told him about falling in love with Alex was completely mind-blowing. Surely, he wasn't acting like love-struck Derek, was he?

In that moment, Rafe knew that Derek was right. And his previously well-ordered world was suddenly tossed on its head.

When the men entered the kitchen, April and Alex were sitting at the table, with cups of coffee in front of them.

"Are you two finished being cops for the time being?" Alex asked.

"We're done for the moment."

Alex moved to Rafe's side and gave him a hug. "Be careful, brother. And take your pills. I want you to try to stay off that leg tonight."

"I've got stock to feed."

"I'm sure April would be glad to do it for you."

"No," both Derek and Rafe answered.

"I'll send Billy Mayer's son out to do your evening

chores," Derek offered. "I'm sure the kid would appreciate the money. He's wanting to buy a used car."

Rafe nodded. "Sounds good."

With a final nod to April, Derek and Alex left. When they were alone, April turned to Rafe.

"Why do you need to pay someone to do the chores? I'll be happy to do whatever you need done."

"April, whoever shot at us might try again. I don't want to put you in jeopardy."

She stared at him, her eyes wide with fear. "I'm sorry." Her lower lip trembled. "This is all my fault."

Although his leg hurt like hell and he wanted to sit down, he opened his arms and April gingerly slipped into his embrace.

"Don't blame yourself, April. You didn't do anything wrong."

His words made her cry harder. Well, damn, he seemed to do nothing right today.

Yet, even as that thought occurred to him, he remembered April kneeling before him, tears in her eyes, as she looked at his wound. And he experienced the oddest sensation.

Peace. It didn't make sense, but there it was.

"For the next few days, April, you need to stay away from the windows. I don't want you to be a target."

She clutched his shirt and buried her face against his chest.

"Will you do that for me, April?"

He put his fingers under her chin and lifted it. He lightly brushed his mouth over hers, then drew her closer. Suddenly, he didn't want to let her go. But his leg was burning like a brush fire, and he released her.

"I believe I need to sit down."

"Let me help you to the couch."

He nodded and allowed April to help him. When he relaxed against the cushions, he felt powerless. Meeting April's eyes—so full of understanding and compassion—those thoughts disappeared. And it pulled him out of his despair. So this was what it felt like to be cared for, he thought. It was a good feeling.

"Yes, Steve, the bullets should be there tomorrow. Derek's taking them into Saddle to mail," Rafe told his commander.

"Who do you think the shooter was after?"

"He was aiming at the woman."

"But he got you by mistake."

"Yeah, I got in the way."

"I don't like my men being shot at."

"I don't care for it, either, Steve."

He laughed. "I imagine not. How are you doing? You need any more support?"

"No. Derek did a fine job of recovering the bullets. My wound's minor. I don't believe I'll be riding tomorrow, but other than that, I'm fine."

"You know, Rafe, I believe your situation needs some more publicity. How about I call around to see if I can get one of the stations here in Midland, or CNN, interested in the story. We'll get a wider audience to see if we can come up with a name for your mystery lady."

"Sounds good."

Rafe hung up the phone, then noticed April hovering near the door to his study.

"Is everything all right?" she asked.

"Yes. I just talked to my commander and told him what happened. I let him know about the evidence I'm sending to the lab."

She nodded but didn't step into the room. "Does this room make you nervous, April?"

Glancing around the neat room, she swallowed. "Yes."

"Can you identify why this room in particular makes you uneasy?"

Her brow furrowed. "I don't know."

"Derek mentioned to me that you appear nervous every time he comes within a hundred yards of you. You acted that way in his office and at the party yesterday. Also, when we went to Alpine, you were as nervous as a three-legged cat in a room full of dogs when you met Wes. You do realize that you react that way to anyone in the sheriff's department, don't you?"

"I had hoped you wouldn't notice my attacks of nerves."

He folded his arms over his chest. "But you're not nervous with me, are you?"

"No," she answered hurriedly. "I'm not—for some reason."

"But my office makes you uncomfortable?"

She pursed her lips, scanning the area. "Yes," she reluctantly admitted.

"Why is that, do you suppose?"

"I don't know." His desk was uncluttered and the trays filled with papers were organized. "Maybe it's the neatness." Shrugging, she added, "It's odd, because your bathroom is neat, and it doesn't bother me. Of course your kitchen isn't, and that *does* bother me. Maybe that blow to my head has scrambled my brains."

He rubbed his chin. "I don't think so. I think that your mind is trying to send you a message."

"That I don't like neat offices, but do like neat kitchens?"

"That's it, exactly."

"I think you're reaching. I made some more chili. It's ready if you want to eat."

"You bet, I want to eat."

"I can bring it in here, if you want."

"Nope. I can walk."

He was right, but April walked by his side, just in case.

"What are you frowning about?" April asked Rafe as he finished his dinner.

"What?" he asked, startled.

"You were frowning a minute ago."

He leaned back in his chair. "I was just thinking about something Derek said."

"And what was that?"

"That today when Alex and he got here, I called Alex 'sis.'"

"Why would it be so unusual for you to call her that?" She rested her elbows on the table and looked at him.

He heaved a sigh. "I told you about discovering that Alex was my sister after I got to know her as the town's doctor and as Derek's wife. We'd developed a friendship. She was good for Derek and his daughter. When I learned who my father was—well, it shed another light on our relationship. I was kinda uncomfortable with it. I hadn't called her sister until today."

She gathered the dishes and put them in the sink. "How long have you known Alex was your sister?"

Rubbing the back of his neck, he looked at the ceiling. "Close to two years."

She turned to him. "Then I say it's about time."

"You don't cut a guy much slack, do you?"

"I would give my eyeteeth to know if I had kin. Don't blow that off. I don't think that Alex is responsible for the actions of your parents."

"I know it. It's just that my mom went through so much." Memories of his mother and her struggles flooded his mind.

"Why didn't she ever contact your dad once she knew where he was?"

"He was married. And my mom had a lot of pride. She didn't want to go to him begging. She made her own way."

"Why, do you suppose, she never told you who your father was?"

"Because she knew I would've confronted him. There was a lot of anger in me as a youth and if I'd met George then, it would've been explosive. Later…" He shrugged. "I don't know why she didn't tell me. Sometimes, wounds go so deep that you can't talk about them." He picked up his glass of iced tea and took a swallow.

"From what you told me the other day, your mom was very successful in her job," April commented.

"Yeah, she was. And a barrel of dynamite."

"And she liked Cinderella stories. Right?"

Before he could answer, the phone rang. Rafe stood and answered it. "Hello."

"Hi, Rafe, how are you feeling?" Alex asked.

He smiled. "Fine."

"Well, if there are any complications, call, and take your pills," she ordered.

"I promise."

"Take care. You're the only brother I have. I don't want to lose you."

He understood her unspoken meaning—that she was glad that he had finally acknowledged their relationship.

"And I know that J.D. and Toni feel the same way."

The way she said it alerted Rafe that maybe his other sisters knew about this afternoon. It always amazed him that he had three half sisters. George Anderson had always wanted a son, but he kept producing daughters.

"I'm going to keep April inside and not let her get near any windows. We'll try to keep her from harm until we can get a lead on her."

"In the excitement of the afternoon, I forgot to ask if you've heard back from any of the hospitals you faxed April's description to?"

"Nope," he replied. "I'm still waiting on that one, too. I've thrown out enough bait that I hope I catch something—besides someone who wants to shoot April." He felt April tense beside him. His eyes met hers, and he saw the fear in them.

"I'm sure you will," Alex replied, bringing him back to the telephone conversation. "Please be careful."

He found her worry over his safety warming. He wasn't alone in the world. He had family that cared. "I will."

When he hung up, he turned to April. She had been hanging on every word he'd exchanged with his sister. Odd, how that word—sister—had slipped up on him. When had he started thinking of Alex that way? It was a nice feeling.

"I take it that was your sister." There was a glimmer in her eyes.

"She wanted to make sure everyone was okay. And warned us to be careful." He paused, savoring the words. When he glanced at April, he wondered if she had noticed his reaction.

"That's nice." She looked down at her hands and traced an imaginary pattern on the countertop.

Something was bothering her. "What's wrong," he asked.

"I was just thinking it was nice that your sister called, concerned with your safety."

There was something else. "And?"

"And maybe in a couple of days, I'll remember who...." She sucked in her bottom lip. Her pain pulled him to her. Framing her face in his hands, he lightly stroked her cheeks.

"I wish I could guarantee you would remember, but I can't. But maybe...." He lowered his head and brushed his mouth over hers, lightly sipping the nectar that was her. She was sweeter than the first peaches, and warmer than a summer afternoon. When he settled his lips firmly on hers, his hands cupped her head, and he tilted it so he could taste her luscious mouth.

His tongue traced her lips, and she opened up, granting him the access he wanted.

One of his arms slipped around her back, bringing her flush against him. His body reacted instantly to her touch, like a flash fire, and there was no way she could miss his need. But it seemed to further excite her. Her hands had slipped around his waist and she was stroking his back.

He wanted to feel skin. Reaching for her shirt, he unbuttoned the first button and ran his fingers over the smooth skin. Suddenly, he heard the sound of an engine. Instantly alert, he stepped away from April and went to the kitchen window.

"Who is it?" April asked.

"It's Billy's son, Charlie. He's here to do the chores. I'll go out and tell him what needs to be done." When he looked back at her, he saw the longing in her eyes, and knew that if Charlie hadn't come when he had.... He didn't need to finish that thought. He had enough trouble already.

Chapter 9

"Hello," April answered the phone.

"Who is this?" the man demanded.

"Uh, this is Ranger Sanchez's residence."

"Well, it's good to know I've got the right number. For a minute there, I thought I had misdialed. The question now is who are you, little lady?"

"I'm April."

"My daughter told me about you."

"Your daughter?"

"Yes, Alexandra Grey."

"Oh, you're Rafe's father. Well, he's out in the barn with the boy who came out to feed the stock."

"Well, I'm glad he feels well enough to be on his feet. Tell him—"

"He's walking in now, sir. Just a minute." April put her hand over the mouthpiece and said, "Your father is calling." She handed him the telephone.

"Hello."

"Son, your sister told me what happened. Are you okay?" For so many years as a youth, Rafe had wanted a dad. Now that he had one, he didn't quite know how to deal with it.

"Yes. Alex took good care of me."

"Well, she's a damn fine doctor. But what is going on there?"

Rafe explained about April and the newspaper article that appeared that morning. "I think it triggered this incident."

"Can't say I'm crazy about your methods," George groused.

"I'm not thrilled, either. But when April wasn't appearing on any missing persons list, I went with a public airing of her story. It brought results."

"But nothing you can't get a handle on." There was pride in his father's voice.

That pleased Rafe. It also surprised him. "I also sent some faxes on April to the hospitals in the state."

"Why'd you do that?"

"Alex told me that April has a distinct scar that maybe a surgeon might recognize, so we're keeping our fingers crossed."

"I can have my secretary call around the hospitals here if you like."

"No, George, this type of surgery is only done at larger hospitals."

"Well, it's good that you and your sister are working together."

"How are you feeling today?" Rafe asked. George had just recovered from a car accident that had killed his second wife. And as much as he was conflicted about his father, Rafe enjoyed the brassy old man. He was the kind of oilman who could arm-wrestle a bull and come out victorious. And Rafe was sure George had done just that.

"I'm doing okay. Your sister, Toni, decided to move back to Midland from Austin. She's going to teach at the university."

Rafe wasn't too surprised that Toni had moved back home. Of all George's children, she was the closest to their father. "Well, I'm glad to hear she's teaching there. I know she'll do a good job."

"Well, if you want any help with your lost lady, let me know. I've got connections."

Rafe couldn't help but smile. His father had enough audacity for two men. But that was probably what made George a success in the maverick business of wildcatting.

"Thanks for the offer." Rafe didn't call him "dad." He might be able to refer to Alex as his sister, but he still wasn't ready for that next step.

April was watching him when he hung up the phone. "You call your father 'George'?"

"I do. Apparently, Alex called him and told him about the shooting. He was concerned."

"That was nice of him."

Rafe shrugged. "I guess." That was as much credit as he could give George.

"How did it go with the evening feeding?" April asked.

"Charlie's a good kid. I paid him and sent him on his way. I'll be well enough to feed the stock tomorrow morning."

She raised an eyebrow, but didn't say anything.

The phone rang again. Rafe reached for it. "Hello."

"Rafe, this is J.D.," said his oldest sister.

"Did Alex call you, too?"

"No, it was Dad. He told me what happened and about your situation with April. Is there anything I can do?"

"No, thanks." He was truly amazed. He'd met J.D. and her husband, Luke, a detective with the Dallas police department, when they came to Saddle for Alex and Derek's wedding. He'd liked J.D.'s no-nonsense approach to life.

Rafe looked at April. She was watching him, her eyes questioning and worried. He smiled at her, hoping to ease her fears. He grabbed the tablet on the counter and scribbled the word *sister* on it. April nodded.

"Well, if you need me to do anything or check anything, please call."

Having sisters—warm and giving and willing to help at a moment's notice—still astounded Rafe after a lifetime of being alone. This was not the first time they had offered to help him. "I will. Thanks." He hung up the phone and shook his head.

"What did Alex say?" April asked, stepping forward.

Rafe sat down on one of the kitchen chairs. His leg was starting to throb. "That wasn't Alex."

"But you wrote 'sister.'"

He held up three fingers. "You forget I have three sisters. That was the oldest of them, J.D."

"The attorney," she answered quickly.

Rafe threw her a sharp gaze.

"You told me that she was a lawyer that first afternoon at Mabel's."

It was obvious that April's memory since she woke up was working well. "She got a call from George. She wanted to see if she could help. Asked if her husband, a cop in Dallas, could help."

April rested her hip against the wooden base of the counter island. "That was nice of her."

The lady had nice curves. Well, there was something that hadn't been wounded this afternoon: his attraction to April. Rafe grinned. "They make quite a pair," he commented, bringing his mind back to the conversation. "She's a defense attorney, and they don't see eye to eye on many things."

April grinned. "I'm surprised they got together."

He shook his head, thinking of the verbal sparring he'd witnessed between J.D. and Luke. And yet, there was mutual respect between them. And love. That was what blew him away about the relationship. "They were surprised, too. Sometimes sexual attraction overwhelms opposites."

The quiet in the room was deafening. Well, he'd stepped in it that time. "My captain is going to try to arrange a TV interview for you with the local Midland station. Or if he can interest CNN and it's a slow news day, we'll get you on coast to coast. The more people who know about you, the greater our chances of discovering who you are."

"I guess." She didn't sound enthusiastic.

"I've put out through DPS that you were here with me. The Rangers around the state are keeping their eyes and ears open."

He saw the tension in her shoulders relax.

The phone rang again. Rafe's brow shot up. "I got one sister left. What do you want to bet?" He picked up the phone. "Hello."

"Hi, Rafe. This is Toni." Rafe laughed and gave April a thumbs-up.

"Is something funny?"

April's eyes were wide as she watched him.

"I'm sorry, Toni. It's just that George, J.D. and Alex have called in the last few minutes. They all were concerned."

"Oh!" Toni laughed.

"It's just not something I'm used to yet—having a concerned family. It's nice."

"Well, we might all fuss and fight with each other, but when the chips are down, we're there. And what I wanted to do is offer my help, whatever I could do. Do you need for me to identify some birds?" she added in a teasing tone. Toni had a Ph.D. in ornithology.

Another laugh worked its way out. He shook his head. "Thanks, Toni. I don't think there's anything you can do and as far as I know, there are no birds involved in the case. But if I come across any, you'll be the first I call."

"Really, if I can help, let me know. Even you famous Texas Rangers need help occasionally."

"And a smart Ranger asks for help when he needs to. I hear that you've moved back to Midland."

"I'm teaching at UT Permian Basin in Odessa, but it's close enough to Dad for all practical purposes."

"How's he doing?"

"He's doing better. He's wanting to run my life again, so I know he's making progress."

"I guess that's a positive sign."

"It is. Although Dad's pushy, when he wasn't after the accident, it worried everyone. I'm glad he's back."

"Thanks for calling, sis." That was a first for him, too. He was amazed that he thought of all three women as his sisters.

When he hung up, April stepped closer. "That was your other sister?"

Rafe nodded. "George said something to her. She was

concerned and offered to help. It was a nice gesture, but unless birds turn up in this case, I don't know what help she could be.''

"Birds?"

"Yeah. She's an ornithologist. George says she's a pain in the butt when she starts talking about migration and how sludge tanks in the oil fields can mess it up."

Her eyes wide, she said, "Oh."

He grinned. "That's not exactly what George says, but *mi madre* didn't allow me to use that kind of language. As a matter of fact, when she worked for one of the judges down there in Brownsville, he was known for his foul mouth—until *she* got the job as his clerk. After a week, she told him if he didn't clean up his language, she would put in for a transfer and let everyone in the courthouse know why she was asking for the change. It was an election year. She didn't have another problem with the man."

"I believe I like your mother's attitude."

"She was tough, but fair."

He stared out the kitchen window, seeing again the spot where the shooter had been. "I want to warn you again, don't get close to any window. I don't want you to make a target of yourself."

Her cheerful mood evaporated. "Do you think whoever shot at us will try again?"

His hand cupped her face. "I can't say. Whoever was trying today made a mess of things. It depends on how desperate he is. And what he doesn't want you to remember."

The expression in her eyes made him regret his unvarnished words. But April needed to know what she was facing. She'd be safer if she was careful.

"I don't want to take a chance that you might be harmed."

Her eyes grew bright, and she swallowed. She bit her lip and opened her mouth to say something, then shook her head. "But what about *your* safety?"

"Don't worry. I'll keep a sharp eye out from now on. I don't plan on being ambushed again."

She didn't look happy with his answer but, thankfully, didn't challenge it.

He had the oddest feeling that things were going to change. And real soon.

Rafe sat by April as they finished watching a TV program about volcanoes. But he didn't see the screen. Instead, his mind was reliving April's reaction in the kitchen, after he'd been shot.

"I'm surprised that you get this program," April said.

Her voice snapped Rafe back to the present. "Satellite dishes have changed the face of this community. We're now connected with the outside world."

She looked back at the screen, and Rafe's mind wandered again to her reaction in the kitchen. When he had asked her about the incident earlier, she had hesitated. She must be withholding something.

"April, will you answer a question for me?"

"Of course."

"This afternoon when I was shot, you had an odd look on your face. What were you thinking?"

She picked at a nonexistent piece of lint on her jeans.

"Did you remember something? Something that you're not wanting to talk about?"

Finally, her green eyes met his. There was fear in those eyes. "When I saw your wound, for a moment there, another scene flashed before my eyes."

Now they were getting somewhere, he thought. "You want to tell me about it?"

"No."

He reached over and lightly stroked the back of April's hand. He didn't rush her, as much as he wanted to. She needed to feel safe, and pushing her wouldn't accomplish his goal.

Finally she said, "There was a man. He was sprawled on the floor. Under him was a carpet red with blood."

From what she was describing, he could see why she might have lost her memory. Hysterical amnesia.

"Can you tell me anything else about the scene? Is there anyone standing around the body? Can you see the room, any of the furnishings?"

She shook her head. "It happened so fast that I just got a glimpse." Her face was a portrait of misery.

He pulled her into his arms and rested his chin on her head.

"I don't think I want to remember, Rafe, if that's what I saw."

"Don't worry, *querida*. I'm here."

Her lips moved on his neck, gently kissing him. When he looked into her face, there was trust shining in her eyes. Her fingers traced the contour of his chin, then she ran the back of her fingers over his five o'clock shadow.

"Has anyone told you what a handsome man you are?" she quietly asked.

A grin curved his mouth. "Not too many of my fellow Rangers have said anything like that. They say I'm as stubborn as an old mule, or that I can be as contrary as a bear. And there was one guy I was trailing that told me I was as mean as a snake. Of course, Kevin didn't have too much room to talk. He's the gentleman who shot me up a couple of years ago."

She shivered.

"I'm sorry, April. I seem to keep stepping in it with everything I say. Carmen said I had as much finesse as that old bull out in the yard."

"Oh, no." She clutched his hand to her chest. "You've been wonderful. I feel that no matter what happens, I'm safe." Her eyes met his. "There's a strength in you, Rafe. A knowing of right from wrong. And that is rare in this day and age."

Rafe knew he needed to keep her talking. She might reveal something. "I'm not so unusual. Most Rangers are men with well-defined senses of right and wrong. They go with the spirit of the law."

She grinned. "Are you telling me that Rangers aren't real careful with the *letter* of the law?"

"That's a problem that has been corrected." A note of indignation crept into his voice. "Besides, if you can't remember last week, how do you know about those little Ranger incidents?"

"I don't. I guessed it from your expression."

He was dumbfounded by her observation. His wife couldn't read him if he'd carried a placard and she didn't care to try. It appeared that April did.

When April took her evening shower, Rafe went into his office and placed a call to Alex.

"I'm sorry for calling so late, but I have a question for you."

"No problem."

"April's starting to remember things. This afternoon she remembered seeing the body of another man who'd been shot. She can't recall too many details. Is there anything I need to do?"

"Don't pressure her. If she wants to talk, lead her,

but don't force her. Her mind might shut down if she feels she has to remember."

"That's not a lot of help," he grumbled.

"Don't gripe to me, Rafe. You should know that sometimes things take time. You don't get all your leads instantly, do you?"

"No," he admitted reluctantly.

"One thing leads to another. Just look at this experience in the same light. If you're patient, I think April will remember everything."

"I hope it's before that shooter tries again." As he hung up the phone, Rafe realized he had hoped that his sister would have a magical answer. Of course, it wasn't going to be that easy.

When had it ever been?

April wrapped her arms around her waist and looked out the window. She was careful enough to stand back from the window, but she could see the Davis Mountains in the distance on this bright, moonlit night.

In her mind, she relived the events of the day. It had been like riding that roller-coaster that she had seen in her memory. Up—the feeling of Rafe's hands on her ankle as he readjusted her stirrup; down—when Rafe threw her back into his truck, shielding her with his body.

Terror washed through her. Someone wanted her dead. What had she done so wrong? She thought of the body she'd seen in her mind this afternoon. Had she seen something she shouldn't have? Her eyes fluttered closed and she took a deep breath, trying to calm her nerves.

And poor Rafe. He was caught in the middle of her nightmare. She was grateful that his wound had been minor, but it was her fault that he'd been shot, no matter what everyone was trying to tell her.

The flash of memory she had had earlier danced through her brain. Again, she shied away from it. If that was what was in her past, she didn't *want* to remember. And maybe that was the problem.

Up until today, she hadn't given any thought to *why* she couldn't remember. Now, the ugliness of her past had resurfaced and the brief glimpse she had had made her shudder.

Chills raced over her skin. It was going to be a long night.

"Rafe, I've got wonderful news for you."

Captain Banks sounded in a good mood. Rafe was glad that someone was cheerful. Heaven knew, he wasn't. His leg hurt, his head hurt, and each time he looked at April, he started to fantasize.

"Well, I certainly could use some good news."

"There's a CNN crew in Big Bend. They were doing a story on the scum bringing illegals across the border."

"In the park?" Rafe couldn't believe his ears.

"No. They were to meet this informer in a border county, but the guy never showed. So since they were there, they went to the park and did a story on how the *Endangered Species Act* has affected the natural order of things. Well, those fellas are done and going to be driving through Saddle this afternoon. They'd like to stop and do a story about April."

"That's terrific, Steve. Talk about a stroke of good luck."

"Yeah. I told the crew to check in with Derek in town. He can direct them from there."

"I think things are going to start to shake loose," said Rafe, then he hung up the phone.

April was watching him. "What was that about?" she asked.

"You're going to be on TV, April. CNN is sending a crew by the house to interview you. With that much exposure, I think we'll get a lead."

She didn't look thrilled. Wrapping her arms around her waist, she murmured, "I hope so."

April sat in Rafe's study, trying to calmly answer the interviewer's questions. She didn't have much to say. The young man in his late 20s turned to Rafe.

"You found her on your land?" Marty asked, pointing to April.

"Yes. April had been caught in a flash flood. There wasn't any sign of her car and she had no identification with her. We're hoping that if anyone knows her, they'll call the Rangers."

The young man finished his piece and then they shut off the camera.

"When will this run?" Rafe asked.

"We'll file it immediately, but I can't guarantee when it will run. It depends on what kind of news day it is. You were fortunate that we were in the area."

"My boss told me about your aborted story on illegals. That's too bad." Rafe tried to sound casual. He didn't want to alarm the reporter, causing him to clam up. If he pushed, that's what would happen.

The young man rolled up the cable for the microphone. "Yeah, that was an odd deal. The man sounded very urgent. We went down to where he was supposed to meet us, but he never showed."

Rafe wanted to ask more about their informant, but

he knew that the reporter wouldn't give him any more information than he already had.

As he watched the news crew drive away, Rafe's sixth sense kicked up.

Rafe woke with a start. He sat motionless, listening.

A moan floated through the air—the sound of someone in pain.

He threw back the sheet and slipped on his sweats. Then he opened his bedroom door and paused. There it was again—another moan.

"No, no, don't." The echo of the words hadn't even finished reverberating down the hall by the time he burst into April's room.

April's scream tore through the air and she sat up. Rafe crouched and looked around the still room, alert for danger.

No one was there. Except April, who was sobbing.

"April, *querida,* are you okay?" he asked as he sat beside her on the bed.

She struggled to regain her composure, then nodded.

Gently, he stroked back the strands of hair that were plastered to her face. "Can you remember what you dreamt about?"

"Blood. There was so much blood." Her tears began to flow again. He pulled her into his arms and let her cry out her fear. "It was the man I saw earlier today."

He didn't know how much time had passed, but suddenly he became aware of April's cheek resting on his chest, and her soft breasts pressing against him. He tried to concentrate, in spite of the roaring of his blood through his veins.

"Do you remember anything more?"

She paused. "The carpet was one of those oriental ones. Blues and greens. And blood."

"Where is this carpet? Can you see anything else around that stain?"

She pressed her head against his chest, then sighed.

"I know you don't want to try, but I think your mind is trying to tell you something."

Glancing up at him, she said, "I know."

"It sounds logical to me. I've dealt with several amnesia patients who had witnessed something that caused them to lose their memory. Also, it's been a couple of days since I found you. The swelling on your temple is looking better, so...."

She didn't look convinced. After a moment's pause, she nodded. "Okay." Closing her eyes, she concentrated on the dream. "The man is blond. I can't see his face clearly." Again, she pressed her face into Rafe's chest.

"Can you see anything about the man? What's he wearing?"

"A white shirt, tan pants."

"Is there anything else you can tell me?"

"No." She didn't elaborate.

Rafe suspected that she didn't want to recall what she had seen. Maybe later, when she wasn't so frightened and upset. He lightly stroked his hands over her back.

Suddenly, the details of their immediate situation hit him full force. April only had on his T-shirt and her panties. He didn't even have his shirt on, so only the thin fabric of the T-shirt separated them. He could feel every inch of her luscious body.

His fingers ran over her chin and then tilted it up. "Relax, April. You're safe now." He felt like a hypocrite uttering those words; he felt anything but safe and comforting. "There's no one here who will hurt you."

Her eyes locked with his, then her fingers touched his chin. "I believe you." Like a blind woman, she ran her hands across his skin, seeming to enjoy the roughness of his beard. Closing her eyes, she repeated the action. Her lips parted slightly.

"April," he warned.

Slowly as a sleepwalker, she opened her eyes. "What?" she answered absently.

His hand captured hers. "If you keep doing that, I can't guarantee that—"

"Yes?"

"I'm a man. And you are a woman I find very attractive."

"Really?"

His head lowered toward hers. "Really," he whispered before he settled his lips on hers. Blood roared in his ears as he felt her mouth bloom under his. She slipped her arms around his chest, anchoring herself to him. There was no hesitation in her actions. She wanted this.

Her tongue darted into his mouth, then quickly retreated. She didn't have to issue the invitation a second time. Rafe eagerly caressed her lips with his tongue, then slipped inside to taste the honey that was her. Slowly, he ran his tongue over her teeth, stroking the sides of her mouth.

His hands slid down her back and slipped under the T-shirt. Her skin was incredibly smooth, like the finest satin. His hands moved up her back, enjoying the suppleness of her skin.

She seemed as impatient as he was. Her hands skimmed over his back, tracing the bumps of his spine, then eased over the muscles of his shoulders.

He grasped the edge of the T-shirt and pulled it up

and over her head. Pausing, he looked his fill at the beauty revealed to him.

"So beautiful," he whispered and stroked his hand over her fullness. She closed her eyes, reveling in his touch. He smiled at her response. His lips replaced his fingers, and a moan was torn from her throat.

"Do you like that, *querida?*" he asked in a low voice filled with passion.

"Oh, yes." She reached for him and he pulled her toward his chest. The feel of her breasts against him was a brand, burning into his flesh. And it made him feel elemental, like the first man on the earth with his woman. It made him want to bury himself in her warmth and never stop.

That last thought was like a bucket of cold water on him. He closed his eyes and tried to find the frayed end of his self-restraint and honor. April was his responsibility. She wasn't here for him to enjoy for the moment. How could he even have thought that?

She must have felt his emotional withdrawal, because she looked up at him. "What's wrong?" she whispered. "Rafe? Did I do something wrong?" There was a note of panic in her voice.

"No, April," he replied as he set her away from him.

She seemed to feel awkward and grasped the sheet to cover herself.

He stood up. "I'm sorry, April. I had no right to do what I just did. Things got out of hand. I only meant to see if you were all right." He didn't look at her, but instead headed for the door.

"Rafe?" Her soft voice stopped him as effectively as a slug from a .44. But he didn't turn around.

"It wasn't all your fault. You didn't do anything I wasn't willing to do, that I didn't want to do."

Her words didn't ease his conscience. He still felt like a snake.

He turned and looked at her. "It won't happen again, April. If you're worried, don't be."

As he walked out of her room, he thought he heard her say, "I wish it would."

Chapter 10

April stared at the closed door, holding her breath, hoping that it would open again and that Rafe would walk back in. She waited and waited, but the door didn't open.

Sighing, she slid down into her bed. Her breasts were tender and aching. Her eyes fluttered closed and she remembered every moment that she was held in his arms. His chest had been smooth but with muscles that were defined and comforting. The feel of his hard chest under her cheek had given her a sense of peace.

While in his arms, she felt no harm could befall her. Whatever evil lingered in her past couldn't touch her while she was guarded by this Texas Ranger. The terror of her nightmare had vanished the instant he had taken her into his arms.

Although he had reluctantly told her about his family, she wanted to know more about him. What was his favorite food, besides green chili? What kind of music did he like? What was his ex-wife like? And why wasn't there a woman with him now?

She rolled over onto her stomach. She ought to be wondering about her own past, she told herself. Instead she was obsessing about Rafe's, and what he was like in fifth grade. Maybe there was a book in the study. She needed to think about something else besides how attracted she was to a certain quiet Texas Ranger.

She slipped on her jeans and T-shirt and headed toward his office.

Rafe didn't even bother going back into his bedroom. There would be no sleep for him. He walked through the kitchen and out the back door. A soft, cold wind blew down from the mountains. Looking up into the sky, he took a deep breath, hoping to slow the pounding of blood through his veins.

What had just about happened in April's room was something he wanted, but would he be able to pay the price? April was about as helpless as a newborn foal. She didn't need some overzealous cowboy pressing her for sex.

That wasn't what happened, a voice in his head argued.

"Yeah, well it would've if I hadn't come to my senses." He felt as if he were being torn in two. Never before had he run into a case like this, where he couldn't manage to separate his personal feelings from the job. There was no sense of professional distance here.

He muttered a phrase in Spanish, one that would have made his mother wash out his mouth with soap. Turning, he walked back into the kitchen. He paused by the refrigerator, pulled out a plastic jug of water and filled a glass. After downing it, he headed for his bedroom.

When he stepped into the hall, he noticed a light from his office. He knew he hadn't left it on.

He strode into the room, a dozen thoughts racing through his head. The sight of April squinting at the books on his shelves stopped him cold.

"Is there something in particular you're looking for?"

She jumped. "You scared me," she told him.

She hadn't answered his question. And he needed her to answer.

Her cheeks went pink. "I couldn't sleep. I saw some books in here the other day. I thought I might do some reading in the hopes that I could...."

He knew what she didn't finish saying. She wanted something to think about besides the moments they had spent together. He could understand that, and felt like a fool for being suspicious of her. Heaven knew, he could use something, too, to occupy his mind—besides visions of April.

"I have just a few novels. If you like Zane Grey, I have several of his books. I even have a book on Cervantes and *Don Quixote,* but unless you read Spanish, that might not be the best choice for you."

"You read *Don Quixote?*" She sounded as though it was an unheard of thing for a Ranger to have literary taste.

"Most Rangers can read."

She gave him a puzzled frown, then her eyes widened. "No, no I didn't mean that." She sounded nervous. "What I meant was that you read Spanish—I'm making this worse."

He laughed, and she relaxed her stance.

"I also speak Spanish fluently." He pulled the book from the shelf and handed it to her. She opened it up and thumbed through a few pages.

"I read it for a literature class I took in college," he continued. "The DPS always needed Spanish-speaking officers, so I have a minor in Spanish in addition to my law enforcement degree."

"That's wonderful." Her eyes scanned a paragraph, then she handed the book back to him. "I don't think I can read Spanish."

He put the book back. "Then I guess you're limited to Zane Grey. Or I do have several criminology textbooks. They are interesting, but they make bad bedtime reading. And we don't want to add to the nightmares that you had tonight."

"Isn't that the truth?" she murmured.

He couldn't prevent the laugh that burst from his lips. She threw him a glance, then smiled. She took one of the Zane Grey books. He took another.

She looked surprised.

"You're not the only one who needs something to cure insomnia."

"Oh." Her expression told him that she understood exactly what he was talking about.

"Are you hungry? Would you like something to eat?" he asked.

She hesitated, biting her bottom lip. "Well, I could make that chocolate pudding we bought at the store."

Rafe's eyes widened. "Really?"

Nodding her head, she said, "C'mon."

As they walked by his desk, her foot caught the corner of the sofa and she stumbled. Putting out her hand to steady herself, she knocked the neat stack of papers on the edge of the desk onto the floor. Rafe lunged as she struggled to regain her balance. He caught her elbow and steadied her. He felt her tense and looked into her face.

It was clear that she thought he was going to be mad about the mess.

"Are you okay?"

Slowly, she met his eye. After a minute of studying him, she said, "You aren't mad?"

"At what? You accidentally tripping?"

Her glance took in the mess on the floor. "I kind of rearranged your desk."

He was waiting for the punch line, then remembered her question earlier about his being a neat freak. Obviously, she was worried about his reaction. And what was also obvious was that she'd had dealings in her past with someone who would've blown up at such an accident.

He shrugged. "Why don't we pick up this mess, then go have that pudding? I've really got an itch for it."

She stared at him. He ignored her reaction and calmly began to pick up the sheets of paper. When it became apparent to her that he wasn't going to erupt, she helped him.

As she handed him the last few sheets, she smiled at him.

"Thank you."

"For what?"

She opened her mouth, then shook her head. "Just, thank you."

She looked at his chest, and Rafe suddenly became aware of his state of undress.

"Give me a second to put on a shirt, and then I'll join you in the kitchen."

She nodded.

He walked down the hall and disappeared.

April breathed a sigh of relief when she was alone. When she had stumbled into his desk, every nerve in her body had gone on alert, worried about his reaction. Instead of being angry, he'd been understanding and helpful. Whatever she'd been prepared for, that wasn't it.

Taking a deep, steadying breath, April walked into the kitchen. What an odd man Rafe was. Particularly about his office. Yet when she'd messed it up, he hadn't been upset. His reaction was comforting, putting to rest fears she hadn't even known she had.

She was still nervous from the nightmare and her reaction to Rafe holding her. She was drawn to him as a seed in the spring needs sun and rain. She thirsted for him.

Feeling freed from some unknown demon, April walked into the kitchen, trying to remember where she had put the package of instant pudding. Opening the cabinet, she scanned the shelves and found it up on top. Obviously, Rafe had put it up there. Stretching, she tried to reach for it, but she was about five inches too short.

"Here, let me help you." Rafe's voice enfolded her. He easily plucked the box off the top shelf and handed it to her. He didn't move back, but his large body surrounded her, making her sizzlingly aware of every inch of his form.

She noticed he'd put on a T-shirt. She couldn't decide if she was relieved or disappointed. He had an incredible chest, and stomach muscles that were tight and hard. She remembered with clarity how his skin felt under her fingers.

Her breathing sped up as she hung on that precipice of anticipation. She wanted to lean closer and lay her hand on his chest, then raise up on her tiptoes and brush her lips across his. Her desires must have shown in her eyes because he swallowed and stepped away.

She was able to draw a deep breath. "I need to know where your bowls are, and do you have a hand mixer?"

He gave her a blank look, as if she'd asked if he had
an alien from outer space hidden in the kitchen.

"Hand mixer?" He sounded as if he were in a fog.

"You know, it's a machine you hold in your hand,
and it has beaters?"

"Oh." He scratched his head. "I got one from my
mother's kitchen, but I'm not sure where I put it. I don't
have a need for it too often."

"No joke."

He stared at her, then laughed, appreciating her sense
of humor. He walked to a cabinet and opened it. "Let's
see if it's in here."

She shook her head. "I'm sure if I wanted to know
how to fingerprint a man, you could tell me. Or if I
wanted to take evidence from a crime scene, you could
tell me. But you don't know zip about your kitchen."

"You wouldn't take evidence from a crime scene.
You gather it. And if you *did* take evidence from a crime
scene, I'd question why you were doing it."

"See, I told you so." She looked among the small
appliances.

He shrugged. "I guess it depends on what you're interested in."

"Ah, here it is," she called out and lifted it so he
could see. "Do you have any idea where the beaters
are?"

The corner of his mouth twitched. "It's lucky that
Rangers don't have to wrestle with kitchen appliances,
isn't it?"

"That's for sure. But I bet everything on your horse's
saddle is in great shape."

He nodded.

"We're all good at something. I don't expect too
many Rangers are handy in the kitchen. Now, how about

those beaters. 'Cause if you don't have any, you might have to do the pudding.''

He pulled out the utensil drawer, and they carefully went through it, but there were no beaters to be found. In the end, April put the milk and mix in a bowl and told Rafe to stir it vigorously for two minutes. When he was through, he handed the bowl back to her.

"I'll let you take over from here. I've got a reputation to uphold. Why, there's got to be several old-timers whirling in their graves. A Ranger mixing pudding!" He shook his head.

Her laughter rang through the kitchen. "I promise, I won't tell anyone about the victory of the pudding." She poured the pudding into several dishes, then carried them to the table. "Well, let's see how well you did." She took a bite. "It's passable," she teased.

Rafe took a bite. "Well, for a novice, I think I did a decent job."

"You did, but if you'd found the beaters, it would've been a snap."

Motioning toward the kitchen, he said, "Feel free to look for them. Only, I can't guarantee that I brought them back with me from my mother's.''

"Would you like a glass of milk to go with your pudding?" she asked.

He gave her a stern look. "There are just some things that Rangers *don't* do. Milk is one of them."

She bit her lip to keep from giggling. "I'm sorry. I don't know the Ranger rules."

"Well, the milk rule is down there on the list about seventh or eighth."

April stood and poured herself some milk, then returned to the table. "You want to tell me what the other rules are?"

He finished his pudding and threw the spoon in the bowl. "Nope. Those are secret. We don't tell them to non-Rangers."

She smiled. "Is that so?"

"Yeah, so whatcha going to do about it?" He stretched out, lacing his hands behind his head.

The thought came out of nowhere, but the temptation proved to be too unbearable. With lightning-quick speed, she jumped up and began to tickle him under his arms.

Instantly, his arms snapped down and he wrapped them around her waist, pulling her down into his lap. "Oh, so you want to play?" His tone sounded challenging.

"No, I think I'm done."

"I don't think so." And he began to return the favor, tickling her waist. She quickly found out that she was ticklish. More so than Rafe was.

"Oh, stop," she choked between laughs. She was wiggling, trying to escape his fingers. "Remember your wound, Rafe."

He looked at her, then at where she was sitting on his left leg. "Unless you decide to kick me, I'll be okay."

"I wouldn't do that."

His hand cupped her face. "I know that."

April looked into his eyes. All signs of playfulness were gone, replaced by a burning awareness of her. All her senses came roaring to life at the same instant. She felt his arousal under her bottom, saw the thundering of his blood in the veins of his neck, heard the harshness of his breathing as he tried to control his reaction.

But it was that very struggle for control that touched April. It was obvious that he wanted her. She found herself drawn down into the vortex of his passion.

Lightly she traced his bottom lip with her finger, then

risked glancing at him. His eyes were nearly black with desire. Yet, April felt no fear. Only want, and need.

She settled her mouth on his and it was as if she'd opened up a flood gate. The tension she felt in Rafe—his holding back—evaporated, and he turned the full force of his desire on her.

He scooped her up in his arms and carried her to his bed. He laid her down, then followed her onto the mattress. Lightly, he ran his fingers over her cheek, then along her jaw. His hand slipped down her neck, resting at the base, then his lips covered hers.

It was a gentle exploring and tasting, as he made sure that this was what she wanted. And it was. April wanted this passion from him, these strong emotions that she felt stirring in him. With a minimum of fuss, he pulled her T-shirt up and over her head. His shirt also landed on the floor. Her fingers were immediately tracing the ridges of his stomach, making his skin twitch with reaction. His hand settled over hers.

"I want you to enjoy this. If you do too much of that, it will be all over before we start."

His concern touched her deeply. Not only did he desire her, but he wanted her to enjoy this time with him. She smiled.

"I'll try. But touching you is so exciting. And wonderful."

Rafe rested his forehead against hers and breathed deeply, which only added to their awareness of each other. "*Querida,* I'm trying to make this good for you, but each time you open that luscious mouth of yours, you say something that pushes me closer to the edge."

"What do you want me to do with my mouth?"

He groaned. "Such visions."

"I'm not doing anything wrong, am I?"

His head snapped up. "Oh, no. What you are doing is being incredibly sexy and wonderful. So wonderful that I don't know if my heart can take it."

She smiled at him and looped her arms around his neck. "For the first time since I found myself in this situation, I feel whole."

He muttered something under his breath, but then his lips claimed hers, and she didn't worry about anything else but the moment.

His hands skimmed over her body, divesting her of her remaining clothes. His mouth cherished her, tasting and nipping, causing shivers of pleasure to skate along her skin. When his mouth found her breast, April thought she would die from the pleasure that thundered through her. Her fingers sifted through his dark hair, and her heart contracted with emotion. His mouth moved to her other breast, then down to her stomach. When he looked up, the passion in his dark eyes beckoned her. She smiled her agreement. Moving up her body, he entered her. April felt complete.

Joy.

Peace.

When he shouted his completion, she was there with him, falling into the fire, coming out the other side a different person.

If only she knew the person she'd been.

Rafe woke slowly, more relaxed than he'd been since…when? April was in his arms, her body pressed close to his. He'd never before felt such a sense of contentment. And it was all because of the woman he held in his arms.

What they had shared last night had been incredible.

It went beyond simple sex. He couldn't explain it, but there it was.

She sighed as she snuggled closer to him. He grinned, remembering how responsive she'd been. They had made love a second time. Slower, richer, with more care. And he could recall every detail.

Yet in the midst of this bliss, there was one big problem. He didn't know who April was, and she didn't know who she was, either. But the need he'd sensed in her last night had reached out and captured him. He couldn't have denied them.

And yet, as a Ranger sworn to uphold the law, what he'd done didn't easily fall into the arena of acceptable action. Damn, he'd blown it, but what could he have done?

He glanced at the bedside clock. It was past time to feed the stock. Callie would be hungry, and if she wasn't fed on time, the goat tended to be destructive. Lightly kissing April's forehead, Rafe got up and dressed.

With a final look at the woman in his bed, Rafe left the room. If he'd had a choice, he would have climbed back in there with her.

Quit thinking with your zipper, Sanchez, he told himself as he walked outside. There was still a potful of trouble facing them.

April knew the instant that Rafe had left the bed, but she'd been reluctant to confront him, so she pretended to be asleep.

When the door closed quietly, she reached out and pulled Rafe's pillow to her chest. She buried her face in the softness, inhaling deeply. It smelled of man. Visions of last night came in rapid succession along with the feelings that he had aroused in her. They had been so fantastic, beyond her wildest dreams. Or were they? What had been her wildest dreams?

She was a soul without an anchor.

She wanted to believe she would get her memory back and that everything would be okay. She'd turn out to be single, and Rafe would fall madly in love with her, and they would live happily ever after. Well, as far-fetched as that scenario was, if she was going to hope, why not go for broke?

What would happen if she *wasn't* single? What if she was married? And had children? A dread welled up in her heart.

"No, that can't be," she whispered to the empty room.

But in spite of her wants and hopes, there was this black cloud hanging over her head, and a sense of doom. No matter what she wanted, she couldn't ignore the possibility that she had commitments that should be her first allegiance.

She looked around Rafe's room. The pieces of furniture were of dark wood, old and scarred. It looked like Rafe had inherited it from the great-uncle who originally owned this ranch.

On the dresser was a picture of an older woman—no doubt his mother. She was smiling, holding up some award. His mother had been a beautiful woman, with mesmerizing eyes and a beautiful smile.

April glanced around the room for some clothing to put on. It was silly. Rafe had seen her nude, had kissed a great amount of her skin, but she couldn't bring herself to race around his house without a stitch on. She slipped on her T-shirt and left the room. She wanted to be dressed when she met him again. Perhaps clothes would make the meeting a little less awkward.

* * *

Rafe finished throwing out the last of the chicken feed. As he fed each animal, he remembered every detail of last night when April had been with him.

Damn, he had it bad.

He rested his arms on the corral fence and looked out at the distant mountains. Did he regret what had happened between himself and April?

How could you deplore paradise?

But he had this sinking feeling that this paradise had a serpent. The trouble was, he couldn't identify it. But as sure as snakes like to sun themselves, it was going to show up and bite him. The question was, when?

His eyes scanned the horizon, reminding him that there was a shooter out there. Rafe needed to check with the lab and see if they'd gotten the package he sent. He needed to talk to Steve and see if any additional information had turned up. Finally, he had to look at the missing persons lists—again.

When he walked inside, the smell of coffee greeted him. He carefully closed the door after him. April stood at the stove, stirring something.

She glanced up and he saw the wariness in her green eyes. Oh, there was a tension there. Its smell competed with the coffee.

"There's coffee fixed if you want it."

"Okay." As after-the-loving dialogue went, their exchange lacked something.

She nodded. "I hope you like oatmeal."

He wondered how she'd react if he told her he hated oatmeal with a passion. He threw her a glance. "Oatmeal? Where did you find any oatmeal?"

"I got it when we went shopping. Don't you remember? I did buy something besides chocolate."

He rubbed his neck. "Yeah, I seem to remember that."

"I thought that oatmeal would be better for you than eggs again. Cholesterol."

He looked at her in amazement. She was concerned for him.

Rafe leaned back against the counter and took a sip of his coffee. He didn't want to tell April that he'd rather slop pigs with oatmeal than eat it. "Mabel often fixes oatmeal for breakfast and if I'm in Saddle that early, I'll stop by to eat." He didn't mention that he wouldn't order oatmeal.

She nodded. He sensed she wanted to talk about last night, but he decided he wasn't going to be the first person to broach the subject. He didn't have a clue as to how she felt and he was going to wait and see what her reaction was. No sense in shooting himself in the foot if he didn't have to.

You're taking the coward's way out, said the voice in his head.

She dished out two bowls of cereal and put them on the table, then set out the milk. He poured her a cup of coffee and joined her.

A passing stranger would have thought that there were precious jewels in that bowl of oatmeal, the way April looked at it. She didn't meet his eyes.

As they ate, time seemed to drag. Each and every bite of oatmeal was like hot slime in his mouth. He needed to think about something else. It was obvious that April wasn't going to say anything. Rafe decided that if they were going to discuss their loving, he was going to have to bring up the subject himself.

"April."

"Yes." She still wouldn't look at him. Her shoulders were hunched protectively.

He took her hand in his. She tried to resist, but in the end, he won the tug-of-war. "We need to talk about—"

The phone rang. Rafe shook his head, stood and answered the phone. April looked relieved.

"Sanchez here," he answered.

"Rafe, I just got back a report from the FBI," Derek told him. "It came back without a match. Your mystery lady isn't wanted on any federal warrants."

"That's terrific, Derek. Thanks for calling." Rafe hung up the phone, turned and smiled at April. "Your fingerprints aren't on file with the FBI."

"So, I'm not wanted for a crime."

A smile broke across her face and she raced into his arms.

"Oh, I'm so grateful." She buried her face in his chest and took several deep breaths.

His hands stroked her back.

"I still don't have a name."

He tilted her chin up. "Yes, but you've cleared one hurdle. And have one less thing to worry about."

"But what about my dream?"

"Maybe your amnesia isn't only caused by the knock on your head. Maybe you saw something that you couldn't handle, and your mind's way of dealing with the situation is to shut it out."

The color drained from her face.

"That's just a theory."

"But with someone shooting at me, that sounds reasonable, doesn't it?" she added softly.

"It fits."

She backed away from him. "That means I've also put you in danger, haven't I?"

"April, my job is to protect. And what has happened to you is right up my alley."

"But—"

He laid his fingers across her mouth. "But *nothing*. Trust me, April. I'll protect you."

"I just wish I could tell you what you're protecting me from. It would help." She walked back to the table and sat down.

"Rafe, about last night," she began.

He steeled himself. She looked up at him, her eyes huge and dark. "I needed someone. And I think you were kind enough not to leave me alone and hurting. But until I know who I am, I don't think we should do—" she waved her hand "—*that* again."

Well, he'd heard sex referred to by a number of different terms from crude to flowery, but *that* was a new one to him. But she did have a point. One he had been thinking about while he was feeding the stock.

"I agree."

Shock raced across her face. "You do?"

"Yes. It wasn't exactly professional behavior on my part."

"Oh." For someone who'd told him she didn't want to do *that* again, she sounded disappointed he'd agreed.

"Do you want help cleaning up here?" he asked, hoping she'd refuse.

"No."

"Then I'll go check the missing persons reports to see if there's anything new there."

When he left the room, April looked like a child who'd gotten her wish—and wished she hadn't.

April dried the last spoon and pulled out the silverware drawer. What a mess. She pulled out a couple more drawers. Chaos.

Since the afternoon loomed ahead of her, she thought, why not straighten up this jumble?

Walking down the hall, she stopped before the open door of the library. Rafe sat at his desk. Before she could open her mouth, he looked up.

"I was wondering if you'd mind if I reorganized the drawers in the kitchen? You know, put all the silverware in one drawer and the cooking utensils in another."

"Fine with me."

Relief swept over her. It shouldn't have been surprising, but his laid-back attitude was welcome. As she turned to go, his voice stopped her.

"April, why don't you turn on the TV and tune it to CNN in case the piece on you is run?"

"Sounds good to me." On her way to the kitchen, she turned on the TV.

She continued her cleaning. In the third drawer she opened, there was a collection of odds and ends: twine, nuts, bolts, out-of-date warranties, and several envelopes of pictures. April opened the first one, and there before her was a small boy on his tricycle. He was smiling broadly, proud of some deed he'd done. In another photo, a woman was holding the boy. April recognized her as Rafe's mom. And the little boy was obviously Rafe himself.

She went through the other pictures in the envelope. They were snapshots a proud mother had taken of her child.

Eagerly, she opened the next set of pictures. Her hands stilled when she pulled out the first one. They were Rafe's wedding pictures. The wedding couple was attractive. Carmen was a beautiful woman, with eyes that sparkled as she looked up adoringly at Rafe. And he was exceptionally handsome. They appeared to be the perfect couple.

She went through the pictures. They were the traditional ones of the family, mothers, fathers, attendants. Rafe's mother beamed with pride.

"I wondered where those pictures were." Rafe's voice startled April so badly that she dropped the pictures onto the counter. His hand came around her and he picked up the photo of him and Carmen standing in front of the altar.

"She's a beautiful woman, Rafe," April said, unable to help herself.

Rafe held the picture at arm's length. After several moments, he set it down. "I guess so."

She stared at him incredulously.

He glanced down at her. "Do you know what I see when I look at that picture?" he quietly asked.

"No."

"I see a woman who griped and complained that she wasn't getting the creature comforts that she needed and deserved, and how lonely she was, and what a lousy companion I was—always working at the damned job. She wanted the money, and I don't know how she thought I was going to get it. Rob a bank?

"It was the most miserable eighteen months of my life." He took a deep breath, then laughed. "I'm telling you, after Carmen, I think of marriage as a curse."

Well, that certainly smashed any fantasies April might have had about a future with Rafe.

He motioned to the stack of envelopes on the counter. "Are these all pictures of the wedding?"

"No." She pulled out the first one she'd looked at and handed it to him. "These are pictures of you."

He raised an eyebrow, but he didn't say anything. Pulling out the photos, he slowly went through the stack. He came to the picture of himself on the tricycle, smiling into the camera.

"That's my favorite," she commented, reaching out to touch the picture. "You look mighty proud of yourself. What had happened?"

"I had just gotten the tricycle. I was feeling like a grown-up." He shook his head. "It's amazing the things that make us happy when we're young." His eyes met hers, and he added softly, "But you don't have those memories, do you, April?"

"No."

"Coming up on CNN news—the story of a woman without a past. Maybe you can identify her," said a commentator.

Immediately, Rafe and April's attention focused on the TV.

"That's terrific," he said. "I was expecting several days' wait."

They both walked into the living room and sat on the sofa. After the commercial, the piece documenting April's predicament ran. Once it was over, Rafe sat back. "Let's pray that it will bring some results."

"I hope it brings the results we want," April murmured as she walked back into the kitchen.

He snagged her arm. "You said you trusted me, didn't you, April?"

"I do. It's just that I don't like being the center of attention. Makes me feel like I'm standing there in my underwear. It's not a good feeling."

He tucked a strand of hair behind her ear. "That's quite a picture."

"You know what I mean. I feel vulnerable."

"I know. And if anything else was working, I wouldn't have done the TV interview. But we have to take advantage of the opportunities that come our way."

She nodded, but from her expression, it was obvious she didn't like it. He wondered why.

The phone rang about an hour later.

"Rafe," Derek said, "we found the lady's car—or at least we think it's the lady's car. It was in an *arroyo* on the eastern edge of Dick's ranch. He found it when he was out checking his cattle this afternoon. It's a little red foreign job, and it's pretty banged up. I called the wrecker in Alpine to come out and pull it out of the ditch."

"We're leaving right now." After Rafe hung up the phone, he turned to April. "They found your car. Let's go."

They saw the cars parked alongside the road, and Rafe parked his pickup behind the sheriff's car. After helping April out of the truck, he walked with her to the edge of the *arroyo*.

"Hey, Rafe, how's it going?" Dick asked.

"Things are clicking, Dick."

"I heard that you did a television spot about April," he commented, glancing at her.

"Sure did. We're hoping we can get some more leads. Maybe we'll discover something new from the car."

Dick shook his head. "I don't know. It's pretty beat up. I don't see a license plate on the back, but then again, there isn't a bumper to hang a tag onto."

Sure enough, the little car was battered, missing the doors and rear bumper. The trunk had been sprung and flapped open.

April came to the edge of the *arroyo* and looked down at the wrecked car, then at Rafe. Derek was at the bottom, looking into the car.

"It's like someone took a sledgehammer to it and went nuts," April mumbled. All the windows were broken.

"I think you're lucky you weren't in that car when it got caught in the flash flood."

April shivered at Rafe's words. She wrapped her arms around her middle and watched as Derek reached through the broken passenger's window into the glove compartment. "Damn, there's nothing here." He glanced in both the front seat and back seat for the insurance papers. "There's nothing here now." Derek started back up to the top of the trench, then paused long enough to look at the front of the car. "There's no license—no bumper on the front, either."

"How can we be sure it was my car?"

Rafe looked at her. "We'll locate the Vehicle Identification Number on it and run it through the state's computer. Hopefully, something will come back."

"How long will that take?" She looked at Rafe, then Derek.

"We can get that info today—tomorrow morning at the latest."

"But that doesn't tell me what I was doing on that stretch of road," she said.

"I think, April, from the clues you've given me, you were looking for me," Rafe answered. The longer he had thought about it, the surer he was that she had come searching for him. Though he had yet to figure out why.

She didn't argue with him, but watched in silence when the wrecker arrived and pulled her car out of the ditch.

Once the car was secured on the wrecker, the driver gave April his card. "I'll keep it in the salvage yard 'til you make up your mind what to do."

From the look on April's face, it was obvious that she was overwhelmed with the situation.

"Thanks, Frank," Rafe answered. "We'll be in touch in a couple of days."

The man nodded, got in his truck, and drove off.

"Well, I hope y'all are hungry. Alex has dinner waiting for us," Derek informed them.

Glancing at April, Rafe asked, "Would you like a break from your cooking? And some pleasant company?"

"Sounds good."

"All right, Derek, we'll be there." Rafe turned to Dick and shook his hand. "Thanks for your help."

"Hey, that's what neighbors are for." Dick waved at April and Rafe, then hopped in his car and drove off.

April looked down into the *arroyo* and a shiver passed over her. "I'm lucky that I'm alive." The words slipped from her lips. Turning, she said, "And you finding me was a miracle."

He didn't know about the miracle part, but he was beginning to think *he'd* been the lucky one.

After seeing her car, battered the way it had been, a dark cloud settled over April. How had she gotten out of the car? How close had she been—

Rafe laid his hand over hers.

"Quit worrying, April."

Her gaze flew to his. "How did you know that I was—"

"It was written all over your face." He touched the

middle of her forehead. "You tend to get a wrinkle right there when you worry."

His answer surprised her. Was she that easy to read? "Well, it's hard not to worry."

"I understand. But I found you and you're okay. You're getting stronger every day and it appears that some of your memory is returning."

He was right. Snatches of her life were beginning to surface. But she didn't just want pieces. She wanted a past—one that she could remember. She wanted to know if what she felt for Rafe was free and clear of complications. How could she live with herself if she was married to someone else?

But oddly enough, he seemed to understand her dilemma and hadn't pushed. She suspected that he was as confused by what had happened between them as she was. It appeared that nothing was going to be easy for them.

"What are you thinking about now?" Rafe softly asked.

A guilty flush stained her cheeks.

"Uh...."

He waited patiently for her to respond.

"I'm glad we found the car."

He threw her a look of disbelief, letting her know that he didn't buy her answer. But he didn't press her.

"What kind of cook is your sister?" April asked, eager to refocus the conversation.

"Well, for a doctor, she's pretty good."

April stared at him. "What's that supposed to mean?"

"Alex isn't as good a cook as Mabel, but considering that her main goal in life was to be a doctor, she turned out to be a real good cook, too."

"That's the oddest compliment I do believe I've ever

heard. She didn't want to learn to cook but is okay now.''

"Now, I didn't say that, April."

"What exactly did I miss?"

He shook his head. "I can see that putting something past you would be difficult."

She shrugged. "I don't know how good I am at reading people, but with you—"

"Yes?" His voice was soft, but she recognized the pit she was about to fall into.

"I seem to know."

He didn't respond verbally, but she felt him withdraw.

They had plunged over the edge already, and both of them desperately wanted to get back to solid ground. The trouble was that each time they said or did something, the ground under them seemed to disintegrate, leaving them grappling to gain their balance.

Before she had time to reply, the town of Saddle came into view. Rafe drove to the last house on the last street of the small town. Oddly enough, a helicopter sat across the road.

April looked questioningly at Rafe.

"It's George."

"George? As in your father?"

He nodded.

April whipped around and stared at the black-and-red helicopter. Sure enough, "Anderson Oil" was written on the tail in red letters.

April's stomach clenched. "Why's your father here?"

Shrugging, Rafe opened his door. "Can't say. But I'm sure we'll know before too long."

She followed him out of the car. "How can you be so blase about this?"

"What can I do? George's a grown man with lots of

money. He does what he wants.'' There was a bleakness in his voice.

She frowned.

''Maybe he wanted to see Alex or the baby,'' he said. ''Or maybe he wanted to make sure you were okay after the shooting,'' suggested April.

Rafe shrugged off that possibility.

April also had a suspicion that the man wanted to see this stranger Rafe had found, but she didn't voice her thoughts.

Rafe walked around his car and took her arm. ''Don't worry, April. George may be loud and pushy, but he's a fair man. And he respects the person who stands up to him. Also, if Toni came with him, I thought I might explain to you that she's my half sister, too, just like Alex. Dad went through several wives. His first wife gave him one daughter, J.D. Wife number two gave him Alex and Toni. George wanted a son.''

''Are you warning me?''

''I am. Don't let him bully you. And don't think he won't try.''

''Terrific,'' she grumbled as they walked to the door.

A girl in her mid-teens with long blonde hair greeted them at the door. ''Uncle Rafe,'' she cried, throwing her arms around his neck and giving him a kiss on the cheek.

''Hi, sweetie,'' he answered, giving the girl a big hug. Sarah was Derek's daughter by his first marriage. Amazingly, his sister Alex had taken her role of stepmother as easily as a bird flies. Rafe stepped back, he looked at Sarah. ''My, my, you are growing. Your dad must want to pull his hair out, worrying about the young men who want to date his daughter.''

She giggled, then playfully punched him on the arm.

"Dad said I can't date until I'm at least sixteen. Can you imagine that?"

Rafe grinned. "I share your father's view. Don't be a heartache to him."

Alex entered the room with an older man. "Rafe, you're here." Immediately, she walked to Rafe and gave him a hug.

"Where's Derek?" she asked.

The door opened behind them. "Here I am." Derek hugged Alex, then his daughter Sarah. "I see we have company." Derek nodded toward the older man standing in the living room.

"Dad and Toni came down to check on Rafe and meet the mystery lady," Alex informed him, stepping to his side.

George Anderson shook Derek's hand, then turned to Rafe. There was a smile of pride on the old man's face. "You're looking good, Rafe."

Son. Although George didn't voice the word, it was there, shimmering between them. And pride was in George's eyes when he viewed the tall man that was his son.

Another young woman, in her mid-twenties, strolled into the room. She was carrying a toddler.

"Rafe, I thought I heard you," She walked over to him and hugged him, too. The baby cooed at Rafe and lifted her arms to him. It was obvious that the baby had recently had chicken pox; the lesions were in varying stages of healing.

Much to April's surprise, Rafe took the little girl in his arms. He seemed quite at ease with her.

"How are you, *chica?*" he asked, smiling at the little girl.

April gaped at she watched Rafe nuzzle and play with the toddler.

"It's amazing, isn't it?" Alex said to April. "How Becky can wrap a grown man around her little finger. Sometimes when Derek is playing with her, I have to stop and wonder at the miracle of it all."

Alex looked from April to her family, then shook her head. "I'm sorry, April, I haven't introduced you to my dad and sister." She quickly made the introductions.

The family resemblance was strong. George's heritage was stamped into each of his children. Alex shared his eyes and nose. Toni had his hair coloring and dark eyebrows. Rafe had his father's eyes and stubborn chin.

George pumped April's hand and smiled. "You're much prettier in person than the pictures in the newspaper and on TV."

"Thank you."

"Well, Rafe, what have you discovered about this lady?" George asked, sitting in the lounge chair.

Rafe sat down on the sofa and set Becky in his lap. "We just came across a car out on Dick's ranch. We pulled it out of an *arroyo*. We think it's April's. We need to check the VIN number on it."

"I was just getting ready to run the VIN numbers through the state's computer," Derek informed everyone. "It will only take a few moments."

"Make it fast," Alex told her husband. "Dinner's ready."

Rafe, April, Alex and Derek waved as the helicopter lifted off and headed northeast.

"I feel like I've been through the wringer." April paused and looked around to see if any of the others caught her *faux pas*.

Alex's lips twitched. Rafe and Derek's eyes danced with amusement.

"I didn't mean...uh...what I meant was—"

"That George Anderson is a whirlwind and sometimes the best you can hope for is to survive the encounter." There was still amusement in Derek's tone.

April glanced at Alex, then Rafe, to see their reaction to Derek's words. Neither appeared offended.

"I guess that's the best way to put it. Let's go inside." Alex nodded toward the door. "I'll make some coffee and tell you a couple of stories about our growing up." At the screen door, Alex looked back. "You and Rafe coming?" she asked her husband.

"Why don't you give us a few minutes to discuss business, then we'll join you for coffee and another piece of that cake you got from Mabel."

Rafe watched as the women went inside. Derek waited until they were alone, then asked, "Have you heard back from the lab on the bullet?"

"No. But I'm hoping that spot CNN ran on April will bring results." Rafe crossed his arms. "There's something damn fishy going on here. It's ugly, just waiting for the right moment to pounce."

Derek studied Rafe. "There's a different look in your eyes, friend, when you look at April."

Rafe looked off into the distance. "Damn, is it that obvious?"

"No. But you forget, I walked that trail. And it was hell. I shouldn't have touched Alex when I did. But then again, I'm human. And when I saw a good thing, I didn't let it get away from me."

Rafe faced him. "Yeah, but Alex knew who she was. Neither April nor I know anything about her. And that's

killing me. Did I repeat the same mistake as my dad?''
It was an ugliness that taunted him.

''The only way you'll make the same mistake is by
walking away from April,'' said Derek. ''And I don't
think you'll do that.''

''I may have no choice.''

Chapter 11

April glanced out the kitchen window at the barn door. Where was Rafe? He'd been gone a long time, much longer than it usually took him to feed the stock. When they had arrived back from town, he had gone directly into the barn to feed the animals.

She glanced at the kitchen clock again. Twenty-six minutes had passed since she walked inside and left Rafe alone. April had been nervous and jumpy ever since that piece on her ran on the TV earlier today. Seeing her mangled car hadn't eased her fears. The detour into Saddle for dinner had been a welcome relief. But as they had driven back toward Rafe's ranch, her tension had returned.

Glancing at the kitchen clock again, she realized another five minutes had slipped by and still there was no sign of Rafe. Something was wrong. She could feel it in her bones. Squinting her eyes, she tried to see out into the barn. What was he doing? Had something happened to him?

With dark thoughts filling her brain, she went to the back door, opened it, and called, "Rafe? Are you there?"

The silence chilled her.

"Rafe?"

A moan filled the air, stopping her heart. Then, from the dark shadows of the barn door, she saw a figure stumble.

"Rafe," April cried, running toward him.

As she reached him, an arm wrapped around her neck and jerked her away from Rafe's sprawled form. She couldn't see the man holding her, but she felt a hard object poke into her side.

Without thinking, April jabbed her elbow into her assailant's stomach. Simultaneously, she stomped on the arch of her attacker's foot. He didn't release her, but grunted and fell back into the corral fence. The next thing she knew, her attacker's arms fell away. He howled and dropped his gun. She kicked it out of reach.

The man turned and swatted at the goat on the other side of the fence. When the goat finally released him, the man ran off into the darkness.

For a moment, April was so stunned by what happened that she could only stare at the spot where the man had disappeared.

"April."

Rafe's voice brought her back to the situation. She ran over to him and helped him stand. With her arm around his waist, she helped him inside and to one of the chairs at the kitchen table.

"I'll be back in a moment," she told him. Immediately she went to the phone and called Derek, telling

him what had happened and that Rafe was going to need
to have Alex look at him again. She next went to the
bathroom to get a washcloth, and tried to clean up the
slash on Rafe's forehead.

"You didn't have to call Alex again," Rafe protested
as she cleaned him up.

"Stop griping. If I hadn't, your sister never would've
forgiven me."

Rafe looked at her, his eyes silent and searching. April
blushed at what she had just said. It sounded like she
was expecting to be around for a while, and Rafe had
just told her this afternoon that he wasn't ever going to
repeat his mistake of marrying again. At least that's how
she had interpreted his words.

They didn't have to wait long for Alex and Derek to
show up. Alex rushed into the house, her face filled with
concern.

"How is he?" she asked April.

"When I called, it was bleeding badly. But it's
stopped now and doesn't look too bad. It just frightened
me."

"I'm glad you called, April." Alex set to work examining Rafe.

"Tell me what happened, Rafe," Derek said.

"I was finishing up feeding the horses. When I went
to get the oats, someone hit me on the side of the head.
When I woke up, I staggered out of the barn. Whoever
hit me was still there, and followed me outside. When
April came out of the house, he grabbed her from behind. I can't tell you too much after that. I fell again,
and all I remember is the man yelling and running off."

Derek turned to April. "Why don't you explain why
the man ran off."

"When he grabbed me, I started to fight. I elbowed

him and stomped on his foot. He backed into the corral fence, then howled. I think Callie bit him on his rear end and he dropped his gun. I kicked it away from him. When Callie let him loose, he tore off into the night.''

April felt her cheeks heat as she related the story. There was stunned silence when she finished. Alex snorted as she tried to swallow her laugh, then gave up any attempt to hold back. Derek grinned, and Rafe shook his head.

"Your suspect shouldn't be too hard to find," Alex quipped. "He won't be able to sit and he'll have bite marks on his buttocks."

"Do you think the attempt on April was connected to the last incident?" Derek asked. Derek and Rafe were in his office. The attacker's gun sat on the desk between them.

"Sure. And I think it's more than a coincidence that the piece on CNN ran this afternoon—immediately followed by the second attempt on April's life. I think it's time we moved April."

"Where do you want to go?"

"For tonight, I'd like to drive into Alpine. Ralph Moore—you remember him, he teaches at the university, and does some work for the Rangers—he's traveling overseas with his wife. I'm going to use his house. It has all the computer links and setup that I need. I'd also like to leave my truck here and use Alex's car to drive April there. Is that okay with you?"

"It's fine with me, but you'll need to ask Alex. I learned the hard way not to talk for my wife."

Rafe sat back in his chair. "Stepped in it, did ya?"

"Let's say, I won't repeat that mistake again."

"Assuming that it's okay with Alex, I'll need to forward my calls to the sheriff's office there in Alpine. I'll alert Wes that I'm doing that. I don't want to miss any leads that might come in. I can take this gun with me to Alpine and drop it by Wes's office. He can forward it on to the lab.''

''Sounds reasonable to me. Why don't we go tell the ladies?''

Before they could leave the room, the phone rang. Rafe picked it up. ''Sanchez, here.''

''Ranger Sanchez, my name is David McMillan. I'm a surgeon at San Antonio General. I'm responding to the segment on CNN. I recognized the lady in the picture.''

Blood pounded through Rafe's veins. ''That's terrific, doctor. Can you give me her name?''

''Her name is Lynn A. Carson. She lives in San Antonio. She came to me two years ago for hernia repair surgery.''

''Could you give me her home address and phone number.''

''Sure.'' The doctor rattled off the information.

''Does it list on her chart if she is single or married?''

''Let me see...ah, here it is. Yes, the lady is listed as married.''

If a bomb had exploded in the room, Rafe couldn't have been more stunned. It was like being kicked in the head by a horse; disorientating and painful as landing on a prickly pear.

He gulped. ''Thank you, doctor. I'll be sure the lady gets the information.'' When he hung up, Rafe stared at the phone as if it were a devil from the hell he'd been thrust into.

''Who was that?'' April asked from the doorway. She and Alex were waiting, along with Derek, for news of the call.

What did he tell everyone? The truth—with all its ugly implications? That was his only option.

Steeling himself, he looked at April. "It was a doctor from San Antonio. Apparently, he recognized you as one of his patients."

She came slowly into the room. "It wasn't good news, was it?"

Rafe's poker face failed him. "How could it not be good news? You're Lynn Carson and you live in San Antonio." He gave her the address and her phone number.

April's expression was wary, as if waiting for the other shoe to drop. "What else did he say?"

"Why don't I call the telephone number he gave me?" He didn't look at her.

Alex walked to her husband's side and they watched quietly.

Stepping to the desk, April touched Rafe's shoulder. When he looked at her, she asked, "What else did you ask, Rafe?"

He considered ignoring the question, but one look into her eyes told him he couldn't do that. He cursed under his breath. "Your marital status."

Her shoulders straightened. "I assume from your reaction, the doctor gave it to you."

"Yes." He couldn't bring himself to say more.

"I take it I'm married." Her voice was so soft that it shouldn't have sliced through him as it did, but it left him bleeding.

"We don't even know if this doctor was right. Maybe it was a mistake. Why don't I get into the DPS computer and call up a copy of Lynn Carson's driver's license. That will give us more to go on than just conjecture." He ignored Alex and Derek sitting on the couch. It had to be as obvious as the mountains outside his window that April and he were more than just a lost soul and the Ranger guarding her.

"That sounds good to me." Her voice held a note of hope.

Rafe pulled another chair close to his computer screen.

When she settled next to him, he called up the license for Lynn A. Carson of San Antonio. It took only a few moments, but Rafe lived a lifetime in those seconds. Finally, the machine put up Lynn's license. It was a picture of the woman sitting next to him.

Pointing, she said, "Unless I have a twin, that's me."

Rafe was fighting this each step of the way. "Let's call the phone number the doctor gave us. Maybe there is someone there who could answer our questions about you."

Biting her lower lip, she nodded.

With a sense of dread, Rafe punched in the number the doctor gave him. After the fourth ring, the answering machine clicked on. The woman who recorded the message sounded like April. He pulled the phone away from his ear and let April listen. When the message was over, he hung up.

She glanced at him. "I'm married." Her face had lost all its color.

The visions of last night's ecstasy taunted him, turning pleasure into pain. "At this point, it would appear you are. But remember, when I found you, you didn't have a wedding ring on, nor did it look like you had worn one recently." He glanced at Alex and Derek. Their expression said they sympathized with him. It didn't help. Not one damn bit.

"If I'm married, why didn't my h-husband report me missing?"

That was the question burning through his soul. "That's what I want to know. If you were mine—" There was heat in his words. He ran his fingers through his hair. "We need to leave, April. Derek and I decided after the attempt on your life tonight to move you. There's a safe house in Alpine that I can use. We'll spend the night there. Why don't you go and pack your things?"

She nodded and left the room.

Rafe turned to his sister. "Do you mind if we borrow your car?"

"No. If you want, I'll call Dad and have him send the helicopter to take you to Midland."

"No. This particular safe house has computer, links, and all I need to try to finish tracking down April's— Lynn's identity." He stood and walked to the door. "I need to pack a few things. I'll also need to make arrangements for the animals to be fed."

"I'll do that, Rafe," Derek volunteered.

"Thanks."

Alex walked to the door and wrapped her arms around Rafe's waist, then planted a kiss on his cheek. "Forgive yourself, brother. You're human."

Rafe's gaze locked with Derek's.

"Trust her," Derek answered. "She's been there."

Rafe wished it were that easy.

April glanced around the new Jeep. "I like your sister's taste in cars."

"She has a lot of county to cover."

"She has a cute baby."

"I think Alex was surprised at how much she likes being a mom."

Guilt rode April hard. It was her fault that Rafe was hurt and that he had to leave his home. But what really haunted her was the fact that she might be married. What she was feeling for Rafe at this moment wasn't what a married lady should feel for someone who wasn't her husband.

How could the magic of last night have turned into such horror today? What they had shared had been wondrous, deep and intoxicating. How could it have changed with the light of day?

She closed her eyes and rested her head on the seat. This seemed to be a puzzle with no answer. At least no answer that made sense.

Or one she wanted to hear.

Rafe glanced at April. Her expression of misery mirrored his own. He had wanted to yank the phone from the wall when the doctor had informed him that April was married. That can't be, his mind kept telling him. It simply wasn't right. And yet, if April had a husband—one she'd had a falling out with—maybe the guy wanted to get rid of her, and why not just shoot her?

And yet, that didn't make sense. Divorce was a messy thing, but it was simpler than killing one's spouse. Unless there was something to be gained by the death.

He glanced at April. Maybe that's what was going on. Well, he wasn't going to stop his investigation until he had some answers.

Suddenly, he remembered the stranger that had shown up in town. Maybe if he could get a picture of April's husband, he could have Derek take it to Mabel's and see if she recognized the guy.

It was a long shot, but at this point he was willing to take the odds, praying that they would pay off.

When they arrived in Alpine, Rafe stopped by the sheriff's office and dropped off the gun. After a brief exchange with Wes, Rafe drove to his friend's house close to Sul Ross University. It was in an old neighborhood with sprawling trees. When he pulled into the driveway, he retrieved the hidden key kept in the birdhouse, and then parked the Jeep in the garage. He didn't want people to know anyone was using the house.

Rafe made sure all the curtains were drawn before he allowed April to turn on any lights.

"If you're hungry," Rafe told her after he had stored their clothes in separate bedrooms, "there are frozen dinners, and plenty of soft drinks and instant tea in the kitchen."

"I think I'd like a soft drink."

He nodded, grabbed two cans out of the refrigerator, and handed one to her. There was still a wounded look in her eyes.

"April, I—"

"Rafe, there's nothing for you to be sorry about. I wanted what happened between us." Her lower lip trembled. "Unfortunately, I still want you."

Rafe's mouth went dry. His body hadn't changed its mind since last night, either. He'd gladly take April back to bed, but...damn, not with a married lady.

"Why don't I call the sheriff of Bexar County and the San Antonio police and ask if there's a missing persons report filed on you?"

"Can you do that this late at night?"

"Sure, why not. Most departments nowadays have their lists computerized."

It took Rafe about half an hour to discover that neither the San Antonio police nor the Bexar County sheriff had a missing persons report on Lynn Carson.

"Well, so far we've come up empty." He rubbed his chin. "Now that doesn't make any sense. If I was married to you—" a point he'd already made but couldn't seem to dismiss "—I would've been knocking down the sheriff's door reporting you missing."

"Well, why don't we drive to San Antonio and go to this house where I supposedly live. Maybe someone around the neighborhood will recognize me. It might answer some questions."

"We'll do that tomorrow, but there's just something here that's not setting right with me. Let's do a little more checking about you." What Rafe wanted to know was more about Lynn Carson and the situation surrounding her. "I guess I'm going to need to call you Lynn from here on out."

She shook her head. "No. I don't remember anything. I know it should mean something, but it doesn't. Please call me April. You're all I have. Don't desert me at this stage." She grasped his hand, and her eyes pleaded with him.

They'd gone down this road before and had ended up lost. But try as he might, he couldn't deny her. Lightly, he skimmed the back of his fingers across her cheek. "Okay. Let's see what else we can discover about you."

She looked relieved. "What else is there to know?"

"There's not much more we can do tonight. But first thing tomorrow morning, I'll check the credit bureau in San Antonio—see what they say about Lynn Carson. That is, if it's all right with you. I'll need your permission to make the request."

"Sounds fine to me."

He again called the DPS computer and requested a listing of all the driver's licenses with the address listed on April's driver's license.

"Isn't that only going to show me?" she asked after he hit the enter key.

"We'll see."

The computer put up only Lynn's driver's license.

She turned to him. "See, there's only my driver's license. Why ask the computer that question?"

"I was looking for a Mr. Carson. Nothing shows. That means, April, if you're married, you've got a husband who doesn't share your last name or doesn't live with you."

"Why wouldn't he live with me?"

"For the same reason Carmen doesn't live with me. We're divorced."

Her eyes widened. "Do you think so?"

"At this point, it's a reasonable assumption." He didn't add that it was also his greatest hope.

Rafe looked at his watch. The nightglow numbers told him it was 1:50. He'd been trying to sleep for well over an hour. Each time he closed his eyes, another question would pop into his head. And he didn't like most of the damned answers.

Finally giving up, he threw back the covers and slipped into his jeans. This time, he decided that he'd better put on at least a T-shirt. Last time he'd gone wandering around at night, he had met April, and he remembered in great detail everything that occurred after that.

He walked into the formal dining room where his friend Ralph had a jigsaw puzzle—a mountain scene—spread over the table. It was half finished. Grabbing a can of soda out of the refrigerator, he walked back to the puzzle. Maybe if he concentrated on the puzzle, he could put the questions that were racing around his brain on hold for a while. Later he could come back to them and see them from a fresh perspective.

And maybe he could cool the burning in his blood.

Married.

The thought rolled around in April's brain. It just didn't feel right. How could a person forget she was married? But then again, how could anyone forget who she was? Hadn't she done that?

Turning onto her side, she tried to relax, but visions of the way Rafe loved her last night popped into her mind. His kisses were bone-melting and thrilling, making her long for more. She remembered how his hands—

Gritting her teeth, she tried to make her mind go blank. It took several tries but eventually it worked. She was finally drifting off to sleep when, suddenly, the vision of a man lying on the floor, blood surrounding him, came to her. She shot up like a jack-in-the-box.

Throwing back the covers, she got out of bed. Wasn't there a Milky Way bar in the kitchen? she thought, desperate to give her mind something else to think about. Well, why not ease her mind with a little chocolate? She might not know who she was, but she did know she had a chocolate fetish.

Opening the door to her room, she saw the light coming from the living/dining area. She stepped back in the bedroom, but that chocolate was calling to her. Grabbing her jeans, she slipped them on under Rafe's T-shirt and went out.

Rafe sat at the table searching the puzzle pieces.

"You couldn't sleep either," she said, coming to stand by him.

"Nope." He didn't glance at her, but kept his eyes on the table.

She saw a piece that she knew would fit the gap in the corner of the puzzle. Leaning in front of him, she picked it up. Immediately, April realized her tactical error. By reaching for the piece, she had to lean in front of Rafe. Her breasts and his lips were inches from each other. She froze. She felt every inch of him. His breathing had sped up and she could feel his eyes on her as surely as if he had touched her. Picking up the piece, she put it into place.

"My contribution," she murmured.

He nodded. He may not have said anything, but he was putting out vibes and she was picking them up. Her tuner was dialed into his frequency.

"I think I'll get a drink like yours. And I saw a Milky Way in the kitchen earlier. Do you want me to get you one?"

He looked at her then, and it stole the breath from her body. His eyes burned with want and awareness, but April knew he wouldn't act on his feelings. "Yeah. Chocolate sounds good. I'll indulge."

She knew what he meant, but she also saw the other meaning in his eyes, that if he couldn't have her, he'd indulge in chocolate.

"I'll get it," she murmured, hurrying into the other room. She found the candy bars in the pantry. Grabbing them and a drink, she walked back into the dining room. She set the candy bar beside his elbow, then walked around and settled in the chair opposite his.

He leaned back, tore open the candy wrapper and took

a bite. She followed suit. "Do you like to do jigsaw puzzles?"

"I find them challenging. It's like putting together a good case. All the pieces have to fit. This gives me practice."

She studied him as he put several pieces into place. "Why couldn't you sleep?"

"There are lots of questions in my mind. And they keep chasing themselves like a dog after his tail."

She popped the last of her candy into her mouth. "Such as?"

"The one that keeps coming back to me again and again is why, if you're married, didn't your husband report you missing? That one sticks in my craw. I've been looking at that question from different angles, and coming up with ugly answers. And why doesn't the guy live with you?"

He picked up another piece and tried to fit it at the edge of the picture. After three tries, he found the right spot.

"Another thought that keeps showing up in my mind is your fear of the sheriff's department. How does that fit? Why are you afraid?"

"Have you come up with any answers?"

"The one that keeps cropping up is a crooked sheriff. Someone that you crossed, and he discovered it."

It made sense, she thought. "When I closed my eyes and tried to sleep, I saw the man on the floor," she admitted. "I don't want to see it anymore." Her voice quavered.

Rafe's gaze softened.

"Tell me about yourself, Rafe. What were you like as a boy?"

He leaned back in his chair, a ghost of a smile hovering around his lips. "I was a pain in the butt to my mom. It was just her and me. When I was about eight or nine, my mom's family came into the picture. Her brothers and sisters made an effort to involve her with their lives. Still, they couldn't let their father know they were talking to her.

"But I hated being neither white nor Hispanic. And I blamed Mom, and was mad at everyone. Life wasn't fair. I was angry I didn't have a dad.

"Bastard." The word rang throughout the house. "That's what everyone called me." He paused and stared off into the distance. "I tried to live up to the label. I was the meanest, toughest, baddest SOB in school."

Glancing down, he picked up a puzzle piece. "When I was 14, I got caught breaking into a store. The sheriff who arrested me knew my mom. And he also saw a kid who needed a role model. So, the sheriff asked the judge to let me work off my sentence by working for him for the summer." He shook his head. "I didn't realize at the time, but the best thing in my life was being caught by Sheriff Jacob King."

"What did he do?" she asked.

"He worked me to death that summer. I cleaned the jail, ran errands, helped on Saturday night with the drunks who came in and slept off their binges. Jacob was a tough, hard taskmaster—but fair, and he was willing to spend his days off with a sullen kid. He and his wife took me to the beach, to cookouts—made me work, at home and school. Jacob was a man of honor. A man who didn't shave the truth. He was also a man who was faithful to his wife and loved her. It made a big impression on me."

In his words, April heard the affection and admiration he held for the man. "It sounds like it."

"From that time until I left for college, I spent my weekends and free time at the jail. When he died a couple of years ago, I felt like I lost my dad. For all practical purposes, he was my dad." Rafe shook off the memories.

"Of course, when I discovered who my dad was, well—I was madder than hell when I went to Midland. I was ready to tear a strip off George. When I told him who I was, at first he looked like I'd punched him in the stomach. Then he grinned like a drunken sailor. He called in his secretary and introduced me, then had me meet most of the people at his headquarters. He reaction took a lot of the anger out of me."

She smiled. "He confused you, did he?"

"So much so that I didn't know how to act. When all my sisters showed up, that really stunned me. Of course, I already knew Alex.

"I walked away from that weekend mixed up. I was expecting to run into denials and rejection. And I was wanting to hate the man. Instead, I found an accepting family and a man who was proud to acknowledge me as his son. It blew my mind." He picked up another puzzle piece and studied it. "Sometimes, it takes a while to put old ghosts to rest." Glancing at her, he said, "I have only one or two left to bury."

"Peace is nice."

"I hope some day I can say the same thing," he whispered.

Chapter 12

At eight the next morning, Rafe dialed the number for the credit bureau and identified himself as a Texas Ranger trying to track down Lynn Carson. "Do you have any information on this individual?"

"Do you have a court order or the individual's permission?" the woman asked.

"I do. Here, why don't you talk to Lynn." He handed the phone to April and she confirmed that she wanted the information.

It took five minutes, but the woman came back. "It lists Lynn Carson as a good credit risk. Pays her bills. She is listed as a stockbroker."

Rafe was surprised. "Is her marital status listed on the report?"

"Yes. Divorced."

Rafe closed his eyes and took a deep, steadying breath. The weight of guilt lifted off his shoulders. "Is the name of her ex-husband listed?"

"No."

"Thanks for your cooperation." When he hung up the phone, he turned to April.

"An ex-husband." She couldn't help the relieved smile that came to her lips. "I'm divorced?"

"That's what the lady said." He wanted to grin but decided it wasn't appropriate.

Her eyes widened. "Divorced," she breathed. She closed her eyes and her chin dropped. "I'm so glad."

"You're also a stockbroker."

Her eyes flew open. "A stockbroker?"

"There's a data bank that the federal trade commission runs on stockbrokers. Being a law enforcement official, I can tap into it. Let's see what it knows about you." He wanted her permission before he went on.

"All right. Let's look and see."

It took only a few minutes to access that data bank. When he asked for information on Lynn Carson, the computer came back with a picture of April and gave a brief bio on her.

After April read the piece, she glanced at him. "It's odd, but it's like reading about a stranger. I don't feel anything."

"Maybe, but it looks like we're on the right trail."

She stood and walked to the window. "That means I'm free."

He knew instantly what she was talking about. Although he was relieved that he wasn't a home-wrecker, he was still unsettled by this turn of events. These last few hours had turned his well-ordered world upside down, and he had no clue how to proceed from here.

"I feel like I'm on that roller-coaster that I saw in my mind. Up one minute and down the next." She turned to him. "San Antonio. That's where that coaster is. Fiesta Texas."

He stood. "Do you remember anything else. Were you there with someone or can you see anything else?"

Closing her eyes, she wrinkled her brow. "No, there's nothing else."

"But you remembered. That's a positive sign."

She turned back to the window and wrapped her arms around her waist. "Well, then maybe we should go to San Antonio and see this house of mine."

"That sounds good to me. Let me finish a few things in here, then we'll leave."

She hesitated. "All right. I'll be ready when you are."

Rafe stared at the doorway, listening to her footsteps fade down the hall. He felt as if he were riding that roller-coaster along with April. Up one moment, down the next, with no time between the highs and lows to regain his balance.

He called Derek and updated him on what was going on. He also wanted Derek to fax April's fingerprints to the Security Exchange Commission and make sure hers matched those of stockbroker Lynn Carson.

After he hung up, he dialed the number of the company commander in Midland. Steve Banks picked up. Rafe explained what they had discovered.

"Do you need any help?" Steve asked.

"Not at this point. I just wanted to keep you updated. We're driving to San Antonio this afternoon. I need to follow up on a couple of things today. The district attorney in Presidio County is wanting some information before he can prosecute Ames for murdering his wife. I brought the file with me and will fax it to him before I leave."

"I got the evidence that you sent. It's with the lab, but all we're going to do is match it to another casing."

"That's fine."

"Well, I'll keep an eye peeled for anyone looking for the lady. By the way, did you notice on the state missing persons report the listing for Jeff Colby?"

"No, but why does that name sound familiar?"

"He was a deputy in Austin County. His wife reported him missing last week."

Rafe's body tensed. "When last week?" he asked.

"Along about Thursday." That was the day Rafe had found April on his land. "Let me know how things go in San Antonio."

"I will." When Rafe hung up, he stared at the phone. A missing deputy. He immediately called Derek again and told him about the situation. "Why don't you show Mabel the picture of the missing deputy? We might get lucky if that's the guy she saw."

"It's worth a try."

Rafe called up a picture of the man in question. A deputy was missing; reported missing the day after April turned up here. And that CNN crew went down to the border to meet with someone in the know about smuggling illegals. Their source never showed up.

Three coincidences. Rafe didn't like coincidences. And he never discounted something that made him edgy.

Rafe studied the picture on the computer screen. He printed it out. Picking up the piece of paper, he stared at the young man's image.

Should he tell April about this turn of events? He remembered her nightmare of a man sprawled on the floor, bleeding. He hoped and prayed that it wasn't connected to the deputy. Unfortunately, he had the sinking feeling that it was.

"Are you the one who's shooting at April, or are you the man she saw in her dream?" he asked.

Well, the only way he was going to discover if this man had any link with April, he thought, was to let her see it. Turning off the computer, he took the picture and walked to the living room where April was sprawled on the sofa, watching a game show. She looked at him, then sat up straight.

"What's wrong, Rafe?" she asked, carefully examining his face.

His poker face wasn't serving him well around April. It didn't seem he could hide his feelings. "I have something I want you to look at." He placed the picture on the table in front of her. "Do you know this man? Was he the man you saw in your dream?"

April froze and stared at the picture as if she'd seen a ghost. Her eyes met his. "Who is he?"

"He's a missing man out of Austin County. He's a deputy."

"A deputy," she whispered in a strained voice, her eyes going black.

All the times she'd been nervous around a sheriff or deputy came to mind.

She wrapped her arms around her upraised knees and hugged them to her chest. "I don't recall him."

It was obvious that April didn't want to have anything to do with the man. Rafe wanted to push her, but he had the feeling that if he backed off and gave her room, he'd get a better result.

"Are you ready to leave?" He looked at her. She had on a shirt and jeans, but was barefoot.

"I need some shoes." She disappeared down the hall. Rafe folded the picture and put it in his shirt pocket.

There was something going on here, and he would get to the bottom of it.

April took several deep breaths to slow her racing heart. She leaned back against the door of the bedroom she'd used. Although she couldn't exactly remember what the body looked like in her dream, she had a feeling that she didn't want to examine too closely.

When Rafe had shown her that picture, it was as if all the air was sucked out of her lungs, leaving her suspended between life and death.

He was a deputy. The word sent a shiver racing up her spine.

She should tell Rafe about her reaction. But then again, she probably wouldn't have to. He already had seen it and no doubt was wondering why she was acting so skittish. Pulling her crocheted flats out of the suitcase that Rafe had loaned her, she slipped them on her feet. Her ankle was doing much better.

She looked into the mirror over the dresser. She was Lynn A. Carson and had seen the driver's license with her picture on it. That name should mean something to her, but it didn't.

So why did Rafe think she'd be able to recognize the missing deputy of Austin County when she didn't know her own name and couldn't tell him anything about herself? She fought off the depression threatening to envelop her.

What other horrors were waiting for her in her past?

She picked up her suitcase and walked out of the bedroom. Rafe was waiting, and no doubt he had questions. He always did.

Rafe locked the front door to his friend's house and followed April out to his sister's Jeep. He set her suitcase behind the seat, then helped her inside.

As he pulled out of the driveway, he noticed that April's hands were folded in her lap, her fingers tightly interlaced. She'd been as tense as a bow string since she'd seen the picture of the missing deputy.

To him it was obvious that April didn't want to have anything to do with the missing deputy. And her reaction was probably not conscious, but it was there nonetheless.

He pointed to the glove compartment. "I've got a Texas map in there. Why don't you pull it out and read me the distance between Alpine and San Antonio on both 90 and 10." He knew exactly how many miles it was on both routes; he'd traveled them countless times. But April needed something to keep her busy and focused on besides her troubles.

She pulled out the map and looked. "It's shorter on 10," she said after a few minutes.

He nodded. He considered staying on Route 90 since it would take them through Austin County, but Rafe wanted to see April's house in San Antonio before he tackled that mountain. He didn't like going into a situation blind, and if he didn't know about April's life, he would be just begging for trouble.

"Yeah, I believe 10 is quicker. I'll take 67 coming up here and that will get us onto 10."

April stared out her window at the sparse landscape. Her hands were still folded in her lap, but she worried the thumb of one hand with the other. It was obvious that she was anxious.

"What's worrying you, April?" he asked, tired of dancing around the issue.

She looked down at her hands. "That picture you showed me. I don't know if it was the man I saw in my dream. I only remember seeing the back of his head. He was a blond. Was the man in the picture a blond?''

Although the photo had been in black-and-white, the guy's hair color had been listed as blond. "Yes."

"Well, I didn't see the man's face. But when you showed me that man's picture, I had a sinking feeling in my stomach. I don't know why." She shrugged.

"Don't worry about it, April."

She stole a glance at him. He didn't sound surprised at her admission. "You knew, didn't you?"

He nodded. "I had a suspicion."

"But I can't be sure if I knew him. I mean, we just found out that I live in San Antonio. Where was that man from?"

"He was from Austin County on the Texas-Mexico border."

"That's quite a way from San Antonio, isn't it? It's on Route 90, isn't it?"

"It's about three hundred miles, give or take a few."

"So how would I have known him? I mean, you said I sounded like a native Texan who'd grown up around Austin, right?"

"Yes."

"Well, how did I know a man from the border?"

"There are numerous ways in this day and age, April. Rarely do folks stay in the same area where they grew up. Look at me, I grew up in the Valley, yet here I am in west Texas. Hopefully, when we get to your house in San Antonio there will be some clues to help us. Could be that the deputy came from San Antonio to that border county. He could've been the one who moved away. Or maybe you went to that county."

She looked out at the horizon, a frown on her face.

Pieces of the puzzle that were April were coming to him. Too bad he didn't have a clue how to put them together.

"That's the second time you've mentioned growing up in the Valley. How did you end up here in west Texas?" she asked.

"Well, as I told you, after I became a Ranger, my uncle died and left his ranch to me. I'd been a favorite of his and he wanted me to inherit his land. It wasn't hard to get a transfer from Company E to Company D. The hardest part was convincing my wife to move out here."

April turned curious eyes toward him.

Rafe laughed. "What are you staring at?"

"Well, the last time you mentioned your wife, you weren't too—"

"Kind?"

She squirmed on the seat. "That's not exactly the word I would use. You seemed very intense when you mentioned her."

He raised his brow. "Well, I'll tell you something— my ex-wife was a career woman who had no interest in being a wife. She had ambition and none of it was directed my way."

"She was very beautiful."

"Yeah, Carmen was a good-looker. Too bad it didn't go deeper than her skin." His bitterness rang clearly, and that surprised him. He thought he'd put that ghost to rest a long time ago.

"Oh."

"It's amazing how a beautiful face can hide a shallow, callous heart."

Glancing at April, Rafe could tell from the way she bit her bottom lip that she wanted to question him more. Well, he certainly had gotten her out of her doldrums.

Unfortunately, he'd opened his mouth about Carmen—again.

"How long were you married?"

"Five years. And I can tell you, they weren't the best years of my life. Things went from bad to hellish when we moved out here. Carmen didn't like the dust, the weather, the people—there weren't enough and there wasn't a branch of the bank she worked at and there was absolutely nothing for her to do. She rarely had any fun—as if it were my job to make sure she had fun." He broke off his tirade and took a deep breath, trying to regain his composure.

"And I was never home." The words slipped out of his mouth. "It took her only two weeks out here to decide she'd had enough, and she left." He shook his head. "I'm sorry to dump on you. I don't know what has gotten into me."

Her smile eased his guilt. "Don't worry. I don't mind. I certainly have dumped on you, numerous times."

It amazed him that he could say anything about Carmen and sound sane. He hadn't said anything about his ex-wife to another living soul. Not to his mom, relatives, or colleagues. It was too personal. Yet here he was spilling his guts to a virtual stranger. And yet, he couldn't think of April as a stranger. It was almost as if she'd been dropped into his life for a purpose. He just wished he knew what that purpose was.

"It was the best thing for both of us when Carmen decided to leave me. I wasn't what she wanted; she wanted a man who enjoyed partying. And she—well, let's just say, we never agreed on anything, except the divorce. That was the best thing she and I ever did for each other." He laughed and shook his head. "It's amazing how quickly passion can die without anything to support it.''

His words echoed in the truck. He thought about the first months with his ex-wife and the wild nights of furor they'd shared. But oddly enough, nothing he'd shared with Carmen ever came close to the feelings he had during the night with April. Sure, his lovemaking with April had been passionate, but there had been something more there. An understanding. A comfort.

He shied away from that train of thought. "Carmen would've died for sure if she'd known who my father was. Rich oilmen like him weren't her favorites, but she would've liked the money he had.''

"Well, I'll say this for your family, they all seemed to care the other night when they called,'' April said, "and the night I met them.''

Rafe laughed. "It still seems mighty odd to have sisters.'' After a moment he added, "But I think I like it. All the time I was growing up, I envied my cousins their closeness and easiness with each other. I wanted that sense of family, and to my cousins' credit, they tried. But when I met J.D., Toni and Alex, there was an immediate connection. With George bursting at the seams because he finally had a son, I was nervous how my sisters were going to be with me, but they welcomed me with open arms. J.D. even grumbled she wished they had known about me when she was a kid. Then she wouldn't have tried to be the son George didn't have. Toni and Alex agreed.''

"Well, having met Alex and Toni, I look forward to meeting your other sister.''

He hadn't allowed himself to fantasize about the future. Carmen had all but cured him of thinking about tomorrow and what was going to happen. Each day had enough grief for itself, and he had learned not to borrow trouble. But hearing April sound as if she wanted to stick around for a while brought a peace to his soul.

They fell into a comfortable silence. It was a relief that he didn't have to talk every minute—to entertain April.

They stopped for lunch in a diner outside Sheffield that Rafe frequented when he traveled this road. The owner greeted them, showed them to a table and took their orders. Everyone in the restaurant greeted Rafe as if he were an old friend. Rafe, in turn, introduced each one to April. Several of the patrons had seen the piece done on her, but no one knew her.

They were halfway through the meal when the sheriff walked into the café. He immediately walked over to Rafe.

"Rafe, what are you doing in Crockett county?" The man offered Rafe his hand.

"Tom, it's good to see you. April and I were going to San Antonio to see if we can discover something about her past."

Thomas Grant turned to April. The man was in his early 50s, with a charming smile and brown hair that showed gray around the temples. "I didn't see that report on the tube, but my wife did. Have you gotten any leads?"

Rafe explained what they had learned. "We're going to check out the lady's house today."

"Well, it caused talk around here. But then again, we've got our own news story. One of the local girls married a young man who was a deputy in Austin County. The man's been missing for several days."

Rafe rubbed his neck. "Did you know him?"

"I met the kid briefly a couple of years ago before

they moved to Austin County. He seemed a real straight arrow. That's what always puzzled me about the situation.''

A surge of adrenaline washed through Rafe's body. ''Why's that?'' he asked.

''Oh, come on, Rafe. You've never heard about the sheriff of Austin County, Nelson Baker?'' The tone of Tom's voice spoke volumes about his dislike.

Rafe searched his memory for any mention of a Nelson Baker. ''No, I can't say I have.''

''Oh, sure you have. You must have heard of 'Money Bags' Baker, the slickest fingers in the state? Or maybe his other name—the meanest bastard on the border?''

A memory surfaced of a sheriff known for his high living and poor salary. ''Yeah, I think I heard something about a border sheriff living beyond his means.''

A bark of laughter erupted from Tom. ''It's obvious to everyone that Baker is taking money for something, but no one, including the Rangers, has been able to pin anything on this guy. He's slick—slicker than anyone I've ever known. Too bad all that energy isn't directed on the good side of the law.'' He shook his head. ''Of course, there have been a number of border sheriffs that needed to be in the jails they ran instead of outside them.''

Rafe glanced at April. She'd gone whiter than a blazing sun at noon. ''You say he's been under investigation by the Rangers?''

''Yeah, a couple of years, if memory serves me. But they couldn't get anything on him. Heard he was in a nasty divorce. Apparently, the wife couldn't live with him. Of course, it's said that Baker has a violent temper, so who knows what happened.''

''Do you know what happened to the wife?''

"No. She left the county and I don't know where she moved. Of course, I don't keep up with a lot of that, but I can call my wife—see if she remembers about the wife."

"Would you mind doing that for me, Tom. I think it might be important."

"Sure. No problem." Tom stood and walked to the wall phone by the door.

April stared down at her hamburger. Her face seemed lifeless. Lightly, Rafe touched her arm. "April, are you okay?"

She slowly raised her eyes to his. "I think I'm going to be sick. Excuse me." She darted from the table into the women's bathroom.

Rafe had decided to go himself to get April out of the bathroom when Tom sat down again. "I just got a call. I've got to leave. When I talked to Kitty, she said all she'd heard is that the wife went back to San Antonio, where she was from."

Bingo.

"Thanks, Tom. You've been a big help."

"Sure, anytime, Rafe. Tell your lady friend goodbye for me." With a final nod, he walked out.

Rafe went to the phone Tom had used, and dialed Derek to explain what he had just learned. "Why don't you take a picture of Nelson Baker over to Mabel. She might recognize this guy."

"Well, it wasn't Colby who was out here, that's for sure. When I showed Mabel that picture, she was definite that he wasn't the guy."

"This time, Derek, I think we're going to get lucky."

"You got it, Rafe."

When he hung up, April was coming out of the bathroom. Her haunted eyes stood out in her pale face. Step-

ping to her side, he gently cupped her elbow. She
stopped and looked at him.

"Are you finished eating?" he gently asked her.

She nodded.

"Then why don't we go?"

She didn't resist him as he led her to his truck. He
considered trying to talk with her now, but some instinct
told him to wait.

They drove out of town in silence. It was close to an
hour before he saw the first tears roll down April's
cheeks. There was a roadside park at the top of the hill.
He pulled over and stopped the truck. Without preamble,
he gathered her into his arms and held her tightly.

"I still don't remember, but when the sheriff was talking about Nelson Baker, it made me want to throw up.
I got cold and clammy, like someone walked over my
grave." Her gaze lifted to his. "Somehow, I think I
know something about what happened."

"I think you might be right." He didn't want to con-
firm her worst fears, but he didn't see any way around
it. And he wasn't going to lie to her. She had had enough
deception in her life as it was. She didn't need him adding to it.

"Where did the ex-wife go?" she asked quietly.

Rafe pulled back and wiped the moisture from her
face. "San Antonio."

She closed her eyes and rested her head against his
chest. "Oh, it's a nightmare."

He kissed the top of her head. "I'm here, April. I'll
be with you all the way, no matter what we discover."
He raised her chin and looked into her eyes. "Trust
me."

"Yes. I've never doubted you for a minute." A sad
smile appeared on her lips.

"Well, the best thing we can do is go to your house and see what we find there. Hopefully, there will be answers."

She leaned back against the seat and took a deep breath. "Let's go."

The city of San Antonio had grown, so much so that Rafe didn't feel comfortable driving around blind. He stopped at the first convenience store he saw, bought a map of the city, and quickly located the street listed on April's driver's license. It was in an older section of the city—houses mellow with age, lush trees lining the sidewalks.

"Do you recognize any of this?" he asked, looking for the address of April's house.

She bit her lip. "I don't know."

Glancing at her, Rafe noticed the pounding of blood vessels in her neck.

He finally found the address and turned into the driveway of the one-story stucco house. The front yard bloomed with spring blossoms. Color and charm. It fit the woman he'd come to know.

Rafe turned off the engine. "Why don't we go up to the house and see if there's anyone there?" Rafe asked softly.

Her gaze shifted to him. Apprehension colored her green eyes. "Okay."

As they walked toward the door, the next-door neighbor, who was working in her garden, straightened and waved at them.

"Lynn, sweetie, I was wondering when you were coming back. I was so worried about you, I was going to call the police and report you missing." The woman, in her early 40s, wrapped her arms around April and gave her a squeeze. Then she pulled back, her expression turning from joyful to troubled. "What's wrong? Did that ex-husband of yours make your time in Cameron bad?" The woman let out a string of Spanish curses, condemning the man's parentage. "I was worried about you. A snake like him is always no good." She turned to Rafe.

"I'm Elena Cortez, Lynn's neighbor. And you are?"

Rafe held out his hand. "Rafael Sanchez."

Elena's brow shot up. "You got a good one this time, *niña*. Not a sickly pale one like your ex." She shivered. "Where did you meet this good-looking *hombre?*"

"Rafe's a Texas Ranger."

Elena gasped. "A Ranger? Are you sure you want to try another lawman?"

Elena's response confirmed what had, until then, just been speculation.

"*Señora*, we have a bit of a problem. I found Lynn out on my ranch. She was without any identification or memory. We've managed to track her down to this house. Could you help us with her background?"

The woman's eyes widened. "Ah, *niña*, what an awful thing to happen."

"Would you have a key for Lynn's house?"

"Of course. Let me go get it, then we can talk." She rushed into her house.

April turned to him. Terror darkened her eyes. "I don't want to know," she whispered as she rested her head against his chest.

A feeling of protectiveness flooded Rafe. He wanted to save her from this pain, but he knew it was impossible. April needed to be whole, and getting through this valley seemed to be the only way to achieve that goal.

The neighbor emerged from her house. "Here it is,"

she said, holding the key aloft. When she saw Rafe with his arms wrapped around April, she paused, her gaze meeting his.

"I warned her to be careful when she went back to Cameron." She walked to the front door and opened it. Rafe and April followed.

The house was warm and inviting, with plants everywhere. The arched doorways between the rooms spoke of a house built in the mid-forties. The wooden floors gleamed.

They followed Elena into the living room, where she set the key on the coffee table and settled into a chair. "Tell me how this happened."

Rafe explained how he had found April and what had led them to this house. "What can *you* tell me, Elena?"

"Well, Lynn here was going to a wedding in Cameron. A friend she had made when she lived there was getting married and asked her to come. She left ten days ago. She told me she might spend some time with a couple of friends in the county. That's why I didn't get concerned when she wasn't home by Monday. I thought—I'm sorry, Lynn."

April smiled at the charming woman. "It's not your fault."

The older woman shook her head. "I should've known that you going back to that town with that man would be trouble. I had a feeling here." She pointed to her stomach. "Nothing good had ever been connected with him."

"Can you tell me how long you've lived next door to Lynn?"

"All her life. I saw Lynn grow up. Her *madre* died when she was about ten. I helped take care of her. I taught her to cook."

Now Rafe knew how April learned to make green chili.

"When she went to Austin County the first time, she was going down there to talk to the county employees about buying mutual funds for their retirement. And that's when she met Nelson." She waved her hand in the air dramatically. "He was charming, with a smile that resembled an angel. Only you realize that the devil and his demons are also angels. And Nelson Baker is a devil. He put Lynn through hell."

They looked at April. Her bottom lip quivering, she rose and walked to Elena, then knelt down and wrapped her arms around the other woman.

"Thank you, Elena."

"For what?"

April sat back on her heels. "For giving me back my memory."

Chapter 13

They waved goodbye to Elena. As soon as they were alone, Rafe turned to April.

"All your memory is back?" His gaze was wary, as if he couldn't quite believe his ears.

As Elena had talked, things had fallen into place for April: the entire ugly scene she had witnessed in Cameron and the reason why she had traveled to Saddle to find Rafe.

"As Elena told you, I'd gone to a wedding in Cameron. Before I left, when I was getting ready, I found in my jewelry box a broach that belonged to Nelson's mother. It had been passed down for several generations. She had just passed away, and I didn't want to keep it because of all the people in his family, his mother was the kindest to me. Besides, it was a family heirloom. I wasn't part of that family anymore, so I took it with me, intending to give it to Nelson."

She stood and walked to the bookcase in the living

room. Pulling open a drawer, she grasped a photo album and brought it to Rafe. She showed him a picture from her wedding. "That's Nelson's mom there." She pointed to the broach on the woman's dress. "And that's the pin I wanted to return. I mean, although I didn't ever want to see that man again, his mom had always been decent to me."

Looking at the beautiful couple in the picture, it was hard to believe from that bright moment that their lives had turned so dark. Nelson's handsome face hid a black heart.

"The day after my friend's wedding, I drove to Nelson's house with the intention of returning the broach. As I walked to the door, I heard raised voices through the open front windows. When I looked into the front windows, I saw Nelson in the living room, and he was arguing with Jeff Colby." Her blood ran cold with the memory.

"What were they arguing about?" Rafe asked.

She looked at him. His brown eyes held warmth and reassurance, encouraging her to go on with her story. "Jeff mentioned the night that he'd caught several coyotes and the truckload of illegals. The men gave him money, and told him to check with his boss. Jeff was yelling that when he called for backup, no one came. One of the deputies told him to let the group go. Jeff said he was shocked, but did let them go. Jeff demanded to know what the hell was going on."

She took a deep breath, trying to still her racing heart. "Nelson—in that smug tone of voice that I hated so much—told Jeff to quit being such a purist. There were big bucks to be made by looking the other way when the trucks rolled through the county. Nelson told Jeff he could keep all the money that he'd gotten—this time.

Next time, Nelson expected half. He said they could use a good man like Jeff in their operation.''

She shivered, thinking of the words that Nelson had uttered. Other memories of that voice, and the agony that usually accompanied it, invaded her thoughts.

"April." Rafe's voice called her out of the ugliness of her past. "*Querida,* where are you?" The touch of his fingers on her chin made her focus on his face. His warmth and strength pulled her back and eased her heart.

She tried to smile, but she couldn't quite make her mouth turn up. "I was remembering." She shook her head. "But I need to finish telling you what happened. Jeff told Nelson he wasn't for sale, and he wouldn't go along with the plan. That was fine with Nelson, if Jeff kept his trap shut. Jeff told him he wasn't going to swallow the corruption—he would go to the Rangers. Jeff turned to go. Nelson calmly walked over to his desk, pulled out a gun and shot Jeff in the back.''

Even now, the memory of it shook her to her foundations. "I must've made some sound because Nelson looked up. I ran to my car, jumped in and raced off. When I glanced into my rearview mirror, I saw Nelson in the front yard. I knew I was in trouble, and I knew that the best thing for me to do was to report the crime to the Rangers. I didn't doubt for a minute that Nelson would've killed me, too, if he caught me. He never had a conscience. He was always out for himself.''

She reached for Rafe's hand and squeezed. He slipped his arm around her shoulder and pulled her close.

"How did you know where the nearest Ranger was?" Rafe asked.

"When I was married to Nelson, he knew where every Ranger in the state was located. He hated y'all. Thought

Rangers were puffed-up tin gods who thought they were invincible.''

A laugh rumbled through his chest. She glanced up to see Rafe's smile sparkling with delight. "Tin gods who thought they were invincible?"

Her lips twitched. "That was one of the kinder things he said. That's why I knew those old stories about Rangers."

"What happened on your trip to Saddle?" Rafe's calm, deep voice reassured her.

"As you know, there were bad storms that morning. I heard on the radio the warning about flash floods in the area. I remember hearing the roar of the water, and I opened the door of my car. The water hit then, and I don't remember anything until I saw you."

She lifted her eyes to his and saw his burning awareness. His fingers skimmed over her neck. Then his mouth brushed hers—it was the briefest meeting of lips. He pulled her tight against his chest.

"I'm grateful to heaven above that you are safe."

The steady beating of his heart was a comfort. She knew this man would help her and protect her from the wrath of her ex-husband.

Rafe pulled back and lightly kissed her forehead. "I'm going to need to call my commander and tell him what you remembered."

A hint of panic worked its way into her heart. "What's going to happen?"

"Well, after I talk to Steve, we'll probably ask for a court order to see if we can find traces of blood inside Nelson's house. And we'll also want to do testing on his car. If you're going to get rid of a body, you usually throw it in the trunk."

She felt the blood drain from her face. "It would help if you had a body, wouldn't it?"

"It always makes it easier for the DA if we can provide a body. But with your testimony, and the physical evidence, we might get lucky. Also, if your ex was the one shooting at us and trying to kidnap you, he'll have some distinctive bite marks on his butt. That will also help."

"Now that ought to be an interesting warrant."

They laughed. And for April that laughter was a sound of promise.

Rafe walked into the kitchen to phone his boss. April's story about the murder of Jeff Colby had set his teeth on edge. Her ex-husband was a first-class bastard. And Rafe hoped that they could get enough evidence to put him away for a long time.

He dialed Steve Banks in Midland and repeated what April had told him.

Steve's response was short and pithy. "Well, I can't say I'm surprised about Baker. There've been rumors about him for some time. The only problem we've had is catching him with proof that will hold up in court."

"I think what April's provided us with will do the job."

"Okay, I'll call around to see the nearest judge we can trust, and try to get the warrants. You want to luminol the carpet in Nelson's house and the trunk of his car?"

"That's it. Also, remember we want to examine the man's butt."

A laugh rumbled over the phone line. "I can see myself now asking the judge if we can examine the sheriff's butt. I'll try to do it with a straight face."

"I wish I'd seen who knocked me out, but I didn't. April didn't get a good look at the guy, either. Any good defense lawyers will call her memory into question. But if the teeth marks are where we say they are, well, there will be no way around it."

"Court order to look at a man's butt. I think you'll get the award this year for the most unusual request. Give me the number where I can reach you when I get the paperwork done."

Rafe gave him the number at April's house. "I'll be waiting to hear from you."

"I'll put a rush on this."

Hanging up the phone, Rafe sat back in the chair.

"Is everything all right?" April asked from the doorway.

"Steve's going to try to get the court orders. We'll have to wait on him."

"Are you hungry?" she asked.

Several hours had passed since they had stopped for lunch. Rafe's stomach growled with hunger. "I could use something."

"There's a good restaurant down the street. The Mexican food is terrific."

"Sounds good."

In the car, Rafe said, "I'll have to thank Elena for teaching you how to cook green chili."

A soft glow entered April's eyes. "My mom died when I was in sixth grade. Elena took me under her wing and kept me while my dad worked. And she taught me how to cook. I couldn't have asked for a better substitute mother. I also make a mean tortilla."

At the restaurant, after ordering, Rafe asked the question that had been burning inside. "Tell me how you met Nelson."

A sadness entered her eyes as she fingered her tea glass. "Days before I graduated from University of Texas, my dad had a heart attack and died. I was rather lost, alone. I managed to get a job with a brokerage firm here in San Antonio, but the loneliness was a killer. You do things you would never have done in other circumstances. You grab for things you think will make you happy. You believe lies."

His hand grasped hers, and his eyes were understanding.

She paused while the waiter served them dinner.

"Well, about six months after I got the job, they needed someone to go down to Cameron and try to sell the county employees on a retirement plan. I got the nod. I felt that I had taken a major step in being accepted within the firm."

"That's when you met Nelson."

"Yes. Oh, he was charming and charismatic and had me eating out of the palm of his hand before I went back to San Antonio. Well, after about three months of his driving here on the weekends, and flowers and small, thoughtful gifts, he proposed." The expression in her eyes was bleak. "I don't know how I could've been so stupid."

Rafe's hand tightened on hers. "Don't blame yourself, April. I've been there. Sometimes common sense flies out the window and you're left with hormones. It doesn't last long, but when it's happening, you're swept away."

The first genuine smile he'd seen from her today graced her lips.

"We make quite a pair, don't we?" She shook her head.

Rafe reached out and cupped her chin. "We do. In more ways than you know."

Her eyes widened.

"Why don't you finish your meal? I suddenly have an urge to get back to your house."

From the expression on her beautiful face, he knew she understood his meaning perfectly. And he had every intention of loving her today. There would be no shadows this night. No ghosts. Only the two of them—and their passion.

April's heart thudded as they drove back to her house. She loved this neighborhood. She'd grown up here. Knew everyone on the street. Yet, suddenly, the street took on an entirely new look.

Hope.

She glanced at Rafe, then back at the familiar scenery. What he had said to her back at the restaurant had been a promise. They would again know each other. But this time, it would be in the light.

The first time they'd made love, she'd been afraid of the shadows threatening her, the evil hanging over her. Now, it was the promise of heaven.

She swallowed. Her first man had been Nelson. And she quickly learned that sex and love weren't the same thing. It had been a bitter lesson; dreams had been shattered. And yet, her experience with Rafe had been so different. Oddly, not remembering her past lovemaking had freed her to give to Rafe uninhibited by the wounds caused by her ex-husband's callousness.

In the midst of her amnesiac's fears and insecurities, Rafe had made her feel cherished, warm and comforted. But there had been more. There had been a driving force, a racing to a light that had exploded into showers of colored brilliance. And afterwards, there had been a resting of her heart and soul.

This time she could give herself completely—not just as a way of hiding from her fears.

When Rafe stopped the truck in her driveway, she felt suddenly shy. It was silly, but somehow this time with Rafe was like the first. He opened her door and offered his hand. Tenderly, he pulled her from the cab of the truck and tucked her close to his side. They walked arm in arm to the front door.

As soon as they were inside, Rafe turned to April and his mouth captured hers. It was a soft, seeking kiss. He gently coaxed her into relaxing and finding the joy in his touch.

She wound her arms around his neck and stood on tiptoes, fitting her body to his, giving him all that was in her. She wanted to hold back nothing this time. She knew who she was now, that her heart was hers to give. And she wanted Rafe to know that.

He broke off the kiss and took a deep breath. "Ah, *querida*, if you don't want me to take you right here standing against the front door, you'd better not tempt me like that."

She murmured, "That sounds wonderful."

Rafe's eyes went black with his desire. Instantly, his hands slid under her skirt and he slipped off her panty hose and panties. Grasping her around the waist, he whispered, "Put your legs around me." She complied.

His mouth devoured hers; his hips ground against hers. April's hands ran through his hair, then grasped his shoulders. Rafe's hand reached under her skirt to make sure she was ready for him, and he smiled when he felt her welcoming warmth. He unbuckled his pants, readied himself and entered her.

April threw back her head, her eyes closed with the ecstasy.

She had come home. It was a startling revelation.

But before she could consider it, Rafe surged into her again, and all thoughts evaporated. All she could do was hold on while he took her to heights she'd never known existed.

She thought she was going to shatter into a million pieces—and suddenly did. Rafe groaned as he climaxed, then wrapped his arms around her and leaned against the door. His weight and strength were a joy.

It took several minutes for them to catch their breath. Finally, Rafe raised his head and looked deeply into her eyes. "That was unlike anything I've ever experienced. I think the French have a word for it."

"Is there one in Spanish?" she asked, feeling satisfied and saucy.

"I do believe there is." The grin on his face made her laugh.

Before she could say anything else, the phone rang. Rafe raised his brow. "Do you want to get that, or should I?"

"I can, if you let me down."

"And whose idea was this?" he teased.

"I don't recall any complaints." She tried to look dignified as she pulled at her loose skirt. Racing to the kitchen, she picked up the phone. "Hello."

"May I speak to Rafe, please?"

April held out the phone for him. "I think it's your boss."

Taking the phone, Rafe listened. A smile creased his lips. "I understand it was probably awkward explaining to the judge why you needed to see Nelson's butt. But you got it? What time? All right. I'll be there." He hung up. "As you probably heard, we got both warrants. But we're going to serve them at seven a.m. tomorrow."

234 Trusting a Texan

"Oh."

He stepped close to her. "Why the sad face? If we get the blood evidence and the bite marks, it will go a long way to securing a conviction of Nelson for the murder of the deputy."

"But it would be better if you found a body?"

"It's always best when accusing someone of murder if you have a body. But if we don't, what we have come up with is mighty damning."

She looked at his shirt. "Could I come along?"

With a soft touch, he stroked back the hair from her face. "Of course. You have a big stake in seeing Nelson brought to justice, and you should be there."

"Thank you, Rafe."

"For what?"

"For believing in me. For wanting me to have closure to this nightmare."

His fingers stroked over her cheeks, then along her chin. "You've been through a lot. It's only natural for you to want to see this through."

"No, not everyone would think like you do. And for that, you'll always hold a special place in my heart."

His lips brushed hers. "Why don't we go back to your room, and I'll show you in intimate detail how I feel?"

She couldn't prevent the glow that suffused her skin. She grasped his hand and led him to her bedroom.

Rafe wrapped his arm around April's waist and pulled her close to his side. Tasting heaven twice in one day was a heady experience—and one he wanted to repeat again and again.

He closed his eyes and took a deep breath. The air was filled with the intoxicating smells of their lovemaking. And love was definitely what had passed between them. It went beyond the mind-blowing passion that had grabbed him since the first moment he'd laid eyes on April. No, this feeling filled him up, making him want to lay the world at her feet, to fight all her dragons for her, to cherish her and protect her. And to take from her the joy she offered.

And the order.

He grinned.

"What are you thinking about?" she asked. Her fingers danced over the hairs of his chest.

"How organized you are."

She raised up on her elbow. "Me?"

"Wasn't it you who went through my kitchen drawers, mumbling about the mess?"

"Well, they were terrible. I don't know how you ever found anything in that kitchen."

"That's probably because I don't use it. Maybe I need someone in my life who will fix that problem." He waited with baited breath for her reaction.

"A maid could fix that for you."

"I don't want a maid. I want someone who will share my life. Who will be there morning after morning. Someone who will help me feed Callie and the cats. Someone who will listen to me rant about the latest stupid thing the government is mandating. I want a wife."

Her eyes were huge.

"I'm asking you, April, if you'll marry me."

April stunned him by slipping out of bed without answering.

"April?"

"We need to get dressed and leave if we're going to make it to Cameron to serve the warrants. I'm sure you'll need to meet with the other Rangers and coordinate your raid."

"April—"

"I'm getting dressed," she threw over her shoulder as she raced into the bathroom.

Her reaction certainly hadn't been the one he had expected. She had acted as if he'd asked her to jump off a ten-story building. As he slipped on his jeans, Rafe realized that maybe, to her, what he'd asked had been the equivalent of inviting her to make such a jump. After all, her only experience with marriage had been with Nelson.

Maybe there was something to her marriage that she hadn't shared. The thought made him sick.

April's hands shook as she buttoned her shirt and tucked it into her pants. Everything had been wonderful in Rafe's arms. Their lovemaking was incredible, like nothing she'd ever known. But when he asked her to marry him, fear had paralyzed her, draining her heart.

There was another demon hiding in her past.

She looked into the mirror and into her own eyes. Now with crystal clear clarity, she remembered. Tears gathered in her eyes.

She owed it to Rafe to tell him. The question she had was could she overcome the fear and tell him?

It was two in the morning when they left April's house.

Rafe had called Steve and they had decided to rendezvous at a motel at the edge of Cameron. There would be two teams of Rangers, and lab techs to check the carpet in Nelson's house and in his car.

Rafe glanced at April sitting quietly on her side of the truck. From the expression on her face, he knew she wanted to say something.

Rafe didn't push. He wanted to know what was tearing her up inside, but she had to tell him on her own terms. The question was, did she trust him enough to confide in him?

The radio played softly—a love song about a woman who'd left her lover.

"When I was married to Nelson," she began, "immediately after the wedding, I knew something was wrong. He was brittle. Does that make sense?" She glanced at him.

"He didn't like change."

"Yeah. He had to have things done in a certain way. The mayonnaise had to be on the side of the sandwich that was against the meat. The mustard on the other piece of bread. And never, never mix the two. At first, I thought it was a simple quirk. But as time went on, the days were filled with things I could do and things I couldn't. And the things I did had to be done the way Nelson wanted them done. It was like he was draining the life out of me. Wearing me down with his constant, 'You didn't get it right. How many times do I have to tell you how to do it?'"

She shivered as the memories rolled over her.

"April, I'm here." Rafe's voice called her out of the wilderness of the past. She grasped his hand.

"One day, when I had put pickles on his sandwich, Nelson stood, told me what a damn idiot I was, and slapped me across my face." Her eyes met his. "I knew then if I stayed that he'd hit me again. There was never any doubt in my mind. So when he went back to work that day, I packed my bags and drove home to San Antonio.

"When he showed up the next day, he was his old butter-wouldn't-melt-in-his-mouth self. He said he was sorry and it would never happen again. I knew he was lying.

"But the thing that frightened me the most was the other things I knew Nelson was doing. He'd go out and be gone most of the night. When he came back, he had big sums of cash. Regularly, he would go on spending binges, buying me expensive presents. There was no place in Austin County where he could've gotten that much money legally."

"You did the right thing, April." Rafe's voice was a calm place in this storm. "It took guts to leave him. Did he walk away, or did he give you trouble?"

"I told Nelson if he didn't leave me alone, I'd talk to the Rangers about the extra cash that he always seemed to have. He called me some crude names and yelled several threats. Elena called the cops when Nelson started beating on my door. The patrolmen who came talked with Nelson. I don't know what they said, but he left. He filed for divorce first—claimed I'd been unfaithful to him."

"That SOB."

"I was grateful that he chose to let me go. Being blamed was the least of my worries." She stared out the window. "I hadn't seen Nelson from that moment until the time I watched him kill that deputy." Shaking her head, she turned to Rafe. "When you asked me to marry you, I went cold inside. Those times with Nelson crashed back like the surf in a hurricane, nearly drowning me."

"I understand, *querida.* But you need to realize that you can't let Nelson rob you of your life. You must have the courage to go on, to have the courage to live again."

"I want that, Rafe. I really do."

"Then take it."

She wondered if it were really that simple.

Chapter 14

They arrived in Cameron at close to four in the morning. Rafe drove to the motel on the outskirts, where they were to meet with the other Rangers. Rafe glanced over at April, sleeping against the door of the truck.

When he thought about what she'd endured being married to a bully like Nelson, it hardened Rafe's resolve to get the bastard. Hitting a woman was only for cowards, and Nelson fit the bill perfectly.

Rafe glanced at the cars in the parking lot, located Steve's gleaming silver Bronco, and pulled in next to it. The door of the motel room opened and Steve strolled out.

"See you made it in plenty of time," Steve murmured.

"When was the last time I was late for a raid?" Rafe asked, slipping out of the cab.

Steve glanced at the sleeping April. "That the lady in question?"

Stuffing his hands in his back pockets, Rafe nodded. "She wanted to accompany me, to see us confront Nelson."

"Can't say as I blame her. From what everyone has said, this has been coming for a long time."

"Is everyone here?" Rafe asked.

"No. We're waiting on Adams. He's bringing the luminol for the rug." The chemical would tell them if there had been any blood on the rug, even if the sheriff had tried to clean it up.

April moaned, then sat up. "Rafe?"

He leaned down and glanced at her through the window. "I'm here, April. I'd like to introduce you to my boss." He helped her out, then made the introductions.

"It's nice to meet you," April said, holding out her hand.

Steve's hand swallowed April's. "I'm mighty glad to make your acquaintance, April. Why don't we go inside before we attract attention that we don't want. We don't want to tip our hand."

They filed into the rented room. A man was inside sitting at the table, playing a game of solitaire. He glanced up and smiled when he saw Rafe.

"How's it going, Rafe?" the man asked, standing. He nodded to April. "Ma'am. I'm Roger Steel."

The man's manner was cheerful and welcoming and April found herself smiling in return. "It's nice to meet you, Roger. My name is—Lynn."

"Ah, yes, the lady without a memory."

April grimaced. "I unfortunately remember too much."

"I'm sorry that you had to see that murder, but look at it this way, the Rangers welcome the chance to get rid of old Nelson. Guys like him give all law enforcement officials a bad name.''

Rafe slipped his arm around April's shoulder. "I've gotten to know the lady as April, so we've just continued to use that name.''

"No problem," Steve commented.

A yawn caught April by surprise. They hadn't gotten any sleep before they left San Antonio. Rafe's gaze locked with April's and the sizzling awareness that was always there flared. "Why don't you try to catch a little sleep, April. We're going to wait on the last group to get here before we go in around seven.''

She glanced at the bed, then at him. "I think I might do that." Stretching out, she turned on her side and fell asleep.

"I see you're smitten," Steve said quietly when Rafe joined them at the table.

Roger, too, eyed Rafe.

Rafe thought about denying it, but why? Steve and Roger had seen him through the bad days around his divorce.

"I'm that obvious, huh?"

Steve slapped him on the back. "Only to old friends.''

Shaking his head, Rafe said, "It kind of blindsided me. After Carmen, I wasn't looking for anything long term.''

"Oh," Steve muttered. "You're thinking of marriage, again?"

He shook his head. "Yeah. But April is nervous about another law enforcement official.''

"Can't blame her," Roger threw in. "I've heard some stories about this Nelson guy. He's the kind who enjoys being the boss and using his power." He leaned forward.

"But what I don't understand is how he got bitten on the backside?"

Rafe laughed and explained what happened.

While they waited, and as Rafe listened to Roger and Steve discuss several cases they were investigating, Rafe's mind turned to marriage. Both Roger and Steve had had trouble with their marriages. It had been tough going for both men. Steve had managed to work it out with his wife and save their relationship, but Roger hadn't.

Looking at April, Rafe wondered if it was even reasonable to ask her to marry him. Hadn't he learned his lesson with Carmen? She had hated his job and complained that it had taken all his time, leaving none for her. And when they had moved to Saddle, Carmen had a never-ending litany of complaints about the place. It was too lonely. Too flat. Too dry. Too boring. What made him think that April would be able to function there any better? April was a city girl. How would she fare out in west Texas?

Carmen had hated him, and had used his job as an excuse to leave him. Would that happen with April? Would he always wonder when he came home if he'd find April had gone the way Carmen had? Could he survive that?

A knock sounded at the door, bringing him out of his dark thoughts. The last group of Rangers had arrived. As they filed into the room, they glanced at the sleeping woman on the bed. She was a beautiful sight. They turned to Rafe, nodded, then began discussing the strategy for the arrest.

The sound of men's voices greeted April as she woke. She didn't open her eyes, but listened as the men talked about how they would execute the warrant, and who would do what.

As she listened, April was amazed that she had fallen asleep in the midst of these men. She felt at ease around these Rangers. Felt safe. The nightmare of her previous life with Nelson seemed a distant memory. She trusted these men, Rafe in particular.

It was stunning, the realization. Yesterday's shadows were gone. Light filled her heart.

"April." Rafe's soft voice drew her from her thoughts. She opened her eyes and smiled at him.

"Hi," she whispered.

His eyes darkened. "It's time. We're going to execute the warrant. Do you want to come?"

She sat up. "Yes. I didn't come down here to wait in the motel room."

Rafe introduced the other Rangers that had joined them.

"Well, gentlemen," Steve said. "We'll stop by the jail first, and serve the warrant to the sheriff. I believe he's already at his office there. Then team one will test Nelson's car, while team two will test his house. I believe Rafe wants to be the one who examines Nelson's person."

April glanced at Rafe, and in spite of the tension, she grinned.

"Do you want to be there for that, too?" Rafe asked her.

"Naw. I've no desire to see any part of that man."

The men around her laughed. It helped ease the tension that was creeping up her spine.

The three vehicles came to a stop in front of the jail. The five Rangers and April walked in the front door.

The cells were set on the back wall of the large room. There were desks for the deputies in the center area. An enclosed office on the right side was Nelson's.

One deputy stood and looked at April. "Lynn, what are you doing here?"

April remembered the young man as one of the followers who did anything her ex wanted. "Vince. I'm here with these gentlemen."

The deputy turned to the Rangers. "Roger," he nodded to the Ranger he knew. "What's going on here?"

"You need to call Nelson out here," Roger carefully explained. "We've got several warrants to serve."

A murmur raced through the room. Vince walked to the sheriff's office and disappeared. Moments later, he reappeared with Nelson. The man was good looking in an artificial way, and his smile was broad as he walked into the room.

"Gentlemen," Nelson boomed. "What can I do for you?"

Steve handed the warrants to Nelson.

"What's this?"

"We're looking for evidence, Baker. We believe you were instrumental in the disappearance of Jeff Colby."

"And who told you that story?" The words were snapped out. He looked at April.

"We have information that you shot Colby," Steve answered.

Nelson's gaze shifted to April. "I know where you got that misinformation. Well, let me tell you, I wasn't the one who killed Jeff. It was that lady there. Lynn. She came by my house a couple of weeks ago. I heard her arguing with Jeff. The kid was coming onto her. They struggled over his weapon and she shot him. I didn't report it because I wanted to protect Lynn."

Rafe couldn't believe his ears. He had to admit that Nelson was quick on his feet, spinning a story like that out of thin air.

April's face drained of color. "That's a lie," she whispered. "It was Nelson who shot Jeff. They were arguing about the payoffs the coyotes were giving certain people in the sheriff's office."

As quick as a rattlesnake, Nelson—his eyes sharp with hate—stepped close to April and grabbed her arm. He leaned close and whispered, "It's too damned bad I missed."

Rafe had had enough. Instantly, he was between Nelson and April. "Take your hands off her," Rafe growled. He burned with a desire to wipe the floor with the bully.

Nelson correctly read the message and stepped back. "Hey, I'll cooperate. And it's my word against hers. I say April was the one who shot Jeff."

Rafe moved between Nelson and April, completely cutting off Nelson's access to her. "I think, Nelson, if a jury had to believe you or Lynn, it wouldn't be any contest. I believe her. Every Ranger in this room believes her. Your exploits are well known in this area of the state, and I think a jury will find your story unbelievable."

"I'll take my chances." But Nelson's voice didn't sound confident.

"Why don't you step into your office, Baker, and I'll do a personal examination of your backside—unless you want to expose yourself here in the main room."

"What the hell do you mean?" Nelson bit off.

"Read the second warrant, Nelson. It's for us to inspect your person for bite marks. Callie, my goat, bit an assailant. I believe that person is you. Shall we go see?''

Several smirks followed them into the sheriff's office.

A couple of hours later, Nelson had been transferred to a jail in the next county. The Rangers didn't know who had cooperated with Nelson and they didn't want to take any chances.

April had sat quietly and watched as the Rangers had served the warrants and interviewed the deputies. Oddly enough, as she sat in the very building that used to give her bad dreams, April felt at ease. In fact, she felt reborn. The bad memories that Lynn Carson had carried were buried. She was free of those ghosts.

April. That's who she was. A whole person.

Another miracle had happened that morning. When Nelson had accused her of murdering Jeff, Rafe had never believed the lie for an instant. Nor had he resorted to brute force to confront Nelson. He had right on his side, and knew what he was about. The fears that had ruled her heart only hours before had been vanquished by Rafe's simple belief in her.

Now the memories of their loving played through her mind. What they had shared was incredible. Did he want more? she wondered.

Rafe walked into the jail, looking worn and haggard. But when he saw her, he smiled.

''I think we've got most of the ends tied up. You ready to go back home?''

She stood. ''No.''

Surprise flashed across his face.

''You asked me a question last night. I couldn't answer you then, but I can now. Yes.''

Rafe stared at her.

''Yes, I'll marry you.'' She wanted to make sure he understood what she was talking about.

His eyes narrowed. "Are you sure?"

She stepped close and brushed back a lock of hair that lay on his forehead.

"You've managed to lay to rest all the old ghosts in my life. And you've also shown me what I could have with you."

His hands cupped her face. "Ah, *querida,* are you sure you want to take another chance on a lawman?"

"With you, I don't think it's a gamble. You're a sure thing."

His mouth swooped down on hers, letting her know that he was all for the idea.

Applause broke out. Rafe and April looked around at the Rangers and deputies in the room. Steve gave them a thumbs up.

Rafe pulled her out of the building. "Steve, I'm taking a few days off. I'm getting married."

"Take your time."

Rafe smiled at April. "I intend to. Believe me, I plan to take this slow and easy."

April shivered at the promise.

Epilogue

Rafe fiddled with the cuffs of his suit, then glanced at his watch. It was time. He looked at Derek.

"Let's go."

They stepped out into the sanctuary of the church filled with family and friends. A good number of Rafe's cousins, aunts and uncles had made the trip from the valley to Midland to see him marry. Their happiness for him filled his heart.

All of his sisters and their families were in the audience. They sat on the bride's side, since only Elena, April's neighbor, had shown up for the ceremony.

The music swelled and April came down the center aisle on the arm of George Anderson. When she asked Rafe if he minded his dad giving her away, Rafe had been stunned. But as he watched George walk April toward him, Rafe realized that the last trace of bitterness he felt for George was gone. He looked at his gathered family and numerous friends who had traveled from Saddle and knew a sense of belonging he'd never had before.

When he slipped the simple gold band on April's finger, he couldn't help the smile that crossed his lips. April's fingers trembled as she, in turn, placed a ring on his finger.

The ceremony went quickly. When the minister pronounced them husband and wife, Rafe leaned down and tenderly kissed his bride.

"Forever," he whispered in her ear.

She pulled back and smiled at him. "Forever."

It was a promise. And a blessing.

* * * * *

International bestselling author

JOAN JOHNSTON

continues her wildly popular Hawk's Way miniseries with an all-new, longer-length novel

THE SUBSTITUTE GROOM

HAWK'S WAY

August 1998

Jennifer Wright's hopes and dreams had rested on her summer wedding—until a single moment changed everything. Including the *groom*. Suddenly Jennifer agreed to marry her fiancé's best friend, a darkly handsome Texan she needed—and desperately wanted—almost against her will. But U.S. Air Force Major Colt Whitelaw had sacrificed too much to settle for a marriage of convenience, and that made hiding her passion all the more difficult. And hiding her biggest secret downright impossible…

"Joan Johnston does contemporary Westerns to perfection." —*Publishers Weekly*

Available in August 1998
wherever Silhouette books are sold.

Take 2 bestselling love stories FREE

Plus get a FREE surprise gift!

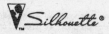

SILHOUETTE·INTIMATE·MOMENTS®
commemorates its

15th Anniversary

15 years of rugged, irresistible heroes!

15 years of warm, wonderful heroines!

15 years of exciting, emotion-filled romance!

In May, June and July 1998 join the celebration as Intimate Moments brings you new stories from some of your favorite authors—authors like:

Marie Ferrarella
Maggie Shayne
Sharon Sala
Beverly Barton
Rachel Lee
Merline Lovelace
and many more!

Don't miss this special event! Look for our distinctive anniversary covers during all three celebration months. Only from Silhouette Intimate Moments, committed to bringing you the best in romance fiction, today, tomorrow—always.

Available at your favorite retail outlet.

Maternity Leave

Coming September 1998

Three delightful stories about the blessings
and surprises of "Labor" Day.

TABLOID BABY by Candace Camp

She was whisked to the hospital in the nick of time....

THE NINE-MONTH KNIGHT
by Cait London

A down-on-her-luck secretary is experiencing
odd little midnight cravings....

THE PATERNITY TEST by Sherryl Woods

The stick turned blue before her
biological clock struck twelve....

*These three special women are very pregnant...and very
single, although they won't be either for too much longer,
because baby—and Daddy—are on their way!*

Available at your favorite retail outlet.